CW00472586

THE VICAR'S WIFE

Emma Hardwick

COPYRIGHT

Title: The Vicar's Wife.

First published in 2021.

ISBN: (Print version)

BOOK CARD

Other books by Emma Hardwick

The Urchin of Walton Hall

Forging the Shilling Girl

The Sailor's Lost Daughters

The Scullery Maid's Salvation

The Widow of the Valley

The Christmas Songbird

The Slum Lady

The Lost Girl's Beacon of Hope

CONTENTS

1

ON THE ROAD TO DEATH

If the Catholic Church had not saved Michael O'Leary, he would've been a boxer, or worse, a brawler on the streets of Dublin.

Michael O'Neil arrived in Kildare in 1847, emaciated and close to death. The Great Hunger had taken its toll on the O'Neil family, and young Michael had to watch his father and mother die on the side of the road while they attempted the walk from Galway to Dublin. The little boy staggered as far as Kildare. He was so desperate for food that he'd begun to catch insects. There was no one to help him. The little child ate them raw. Nobody took pity on him, because Michael was just another ragged child on the torturous road of death. Eventually, he lay down like an animal on the side of the road, and he started eating the grass. Little did he know that his body could not digest it, and although it provided temporary relief from hunger, it gave him no energy, lacking any nutritional value.

The rain was ceaseless, and the sad procession of skeletons shuffled through the beautiful emerald-green countryside, creating a picture of heaven and hell beside each other. Still, the experience was not exclusive to him, millions of his fellow countrymen were travelling the road with him, and they were doing the same things to stay alive. Michael finally collapsed exhausted. He resembled a puppet, all sticks underneath covered by ill-fitting clothes. After days of walking, he found himself a mile out of Kildare, not far from a monastery, the 'White Abbey,' run by Carmelite monks and nuns.

The monks were not much better off than the weary starving travellers. Still, they tried to provide soup made from turnips, cabbage, and bones that they boiled again and again. This sustenance gave the starving masses some comfort on the last steps to their deaths. Rome tried to keep up with the demand for food for their fellow brothers and sisters, but most of the barley, oats, and tea that they supplied were stolen or intercepted by criminals who sold it for an exorbitant price to the desperate. The sick orphans were cared for by the nuns. They were relocated to the abbey, while those who were strong enough continued their journey to the godforsaken poorhouse.

Michael was one of the skeletons that was saved, and he would never forget the first words that he heard.

"He is alive, Brother Andrew. If it's God's will, the boy will live."

The youngster was too weak to talk and finally permitted himself to close his eyes and sleep. It had not occurred to him that he may never wake up again. Instinctively, Michael knew that he was safe and took it for granted that he would survive. He didn't see death on the horizon. He'd the faith of a child.

Michael lay down on the straw bed with a woollen blanket over him. The barn had a fire burning inside a massive hearth surrounded by stone, and it was warm and comforting. For Michael, it was the driest, peaceful place he'd laid his head in weeks. He no longer heard travellers praying for the sins that could have accumulated over the last days of their lives. He no longer heard inconsolable children screeching for food, or the rattled gasping of the dying as they exhaled their last breath.

"Sit up, lad," ordered a woman with a stern but sweet voice.

Michael could not muster the energy to move. He was exhausted and far beyond the point of hunger, in that unpredictable zone, the no man's land between delirium and consciousness. He understood the instruction, but even with his brave determination, all he could do was lay where he was and allow the profound peace of sleep to capture him.

"Brother John," said the stern lady, "sit this here lad up. We must get some food into his body."

He felt strong hands under his armpits. They pulled him into a sitting position and propped him up against a hay bale. His weak eyelids fluttered, and he saw the most beautiful face looking down upon him. Convinced he was dead, it seemed the young nun was an angel in heaven.

Her snow-white habit covered her hair, and her brightest blue eyes bore into his. She'd pale skin, with a shade of colour on her high cheekbones, and she exuded a firm gentleness. She smiled at Michael and made it clear that he'd better follow her instructions, or she would return him to the road where she'd found him.

She'd a wooden bowl of soup in her hand and began to feed him. It tasted like heaven, but after just three spoonfuls, he began to wretch.

> "You haven't eaten for a long time, so I am going to feed you tiny bits at a time, like a baby. We'll begin with a few spoons of broth every hour. I will feed you throughout the night, and by midday tomorrow, your stomach will be capable of more."
>
> "What is your name, lad?" she asked him.
>
> "Michael," he replied, his little face serious. "Michael O'Neil."
>
> "From now on, you can call me Sister Julia."

He nodded. She forced him to swallow three more spoons of soup and threatened to be back in an hour with more. If Michael had the energy, he would've smiled, but he closed his eyes and fell asleep where he lay.

The nun treated him with the utmost kindness, and when he grew sad or afraid, she would put her arms around him and comfort him.

> "Now, now, Michael. We'll look after you. I know that it's difficult without your Ma and Da, but we will do the best that we can."

Sister Julia's prediction was correct, and within twenty-four hours, Michael had the energy to get up. He ate everything she fed him without getting ill. Within five days, he was completely recovered, and within seven days, he was bored. In his childlike capacity, he tried to help the brothers, who were toiling laboriously to produce food for the hungry. They were delighted to include him. Soon, Michael found peace and comfort in his surroundings. He was a young child. Most of the other children that passed through the abbey were either sent to their families in Dublin or the dreaded state orphanages. The orphanages could not facilitate the masses of orphans, and so the older children were shipped off to the colonies as labourers. Still, there remained a constant stream of starving wretches needing help. Because Michael was a robust and cheerful little chap, the nuns and monks became very fond of him. They hid him from the officials relegated to placing children in protective custody. He was blessed to escape the orphanage. Michael worked and played with the monks who became his makeshift fathers, and the nuns became his mothers.

Contrary to popular belief, the abbot was a kindly man, and he instructed the small group of monks to work day and night. He knew their contribution greatly eased the awful suffering of the people who passed through White Abbey. Although Michael was still very young, they taught him how to create a vegetable garden, when to plant the seed and how to preserve what they harvested. He became their favourite with his easy-going nature and lively sense of humour. As Michael grew up, he developed a strong work ethic, and he gained admiration from all the people around him.

The monks realised that Michael needed an education, so amongst themselves, they decided that they would take turns teaching him.

Michael lived at the abbey until in his mid-teens. The abbot, Father Barnabus, was a stoic man in his fifties, and he was convinced that Michael was a hooligan. However, he also recognised Michael's academic potential. Father Barnabus spent a significant amount of time and effort persuading the Roman Catholic Archbishop of Dublin to permit Michael O'Neil to attend the city's prestigious Trinity College.

While Michael attended Trinity, he lived in the confines of the local monastery. Although he was exposed to secular events, he was too busy to take any notice of what happened around him. Michael had no exposure to girls. Thankfully, no women attended the college, so nothing diverted the youth's attention from his books.

By the age of twenty-one, Michael was a well-respected intellectual and had mastered many subjects—theology, mathematics, Latin, Greek, philosophy, law, and ethics. The list was endless. Michael spent a tremendous amount of time spying on the engineers, and he discovered he'd a passion for anything mechanical. He spent as much time as he could afford to watch and try to learn everything. It was unusual for the archbishop to allow such a broad spectrum of disciplines. Yet, by the time that Michael was nineteen, the abbot knew he was intellectually advanced and needed further academic stimulation to keep him from sinful distraction. So, they permitted the young prodigy to attend the University of London to study engineering for a year. The far-sighted archbishop accepted that even the church needed their quota of practical men and that embracing academically progressive ideas during the Industrial Revolution could only work in their favour. This was a far cry from their previous inhibiting policies on wider education. A priest with skills beyond the obvious was always more highly respected, and so, Michael O'Neil went to London.

His religious future would be more predictable. The church would pay for his studies, and he would be ordained as a priest. After his lay years, he would be free to apply for any post in the organisation, clerical or otherwise.

But Michael was a free spirit. His dark skin, black hair and black eyes disguised a rebellious demeanour. He didn't epitomise the typical cleric or embrace the stern discipline that Rome demanded when they ordained a young man into the priesthood.

The bishop had deep reservations about Michael joining the order, and his instincts proved correct. Michael was not particularly pious. He lacked tact and diplomacy. He practised honesty in a manner that regularly threatened his promotion to higher appointments. He spoke it as he saw it. He annoyed a lot of people, yet charmed and endeared himself to others.

Michael was a physical man with practical solutions to complex problems. He acknowledged that he would've had none of these things if not for the church. He owed a debt of gratitude for his education and his quality of life. He believed that he could never fully repay what they'd invested in him, yet he desired to prove himself worthy of their investment—somehow.

2

AN UNORTHODOX PRIEST

Father Michael O'Neil was appointed to the Parish of Bunratty at the tender age of twenty-five.

"Father," said the archbishop, "I am appointing you to a small parish called Bunratty in County Clare."

"Thank you, Your Grace," replied Michael, wondering where on God's green Irish hills Bunratty was.

"It's quite a distance, but you will travel via the abbeys and priories, so food and shelter shall be aplenty."

"I understand this to be my calling, your Grace. Aside from my obvious religious duties, are there any particular issues you need me to take care of?"

"The community is small and poor, Father, and you will be there to give them hope, no more and no less."

Michael bristled. *What good was hope without help?*

With the aid of trains, carts, and horses, Michael O'Neil travelled the one hundred miles to Bunratty.

His driver stopped at the small church, and Michael climbed off the wagon, landing in the ankle-deep mud.

"Thank you, Davey. I will be seeing you around on Sunday, yes?"

"Dunno about that, Father!" Davey yelled above the wind. "You'd better be about your parish business, Father. It's lashing out the heavens, it is," he shouted, water pouring over his oilskins and the brim of his hat.

Father William, the curate, showed Michael to his humble bedroom in the rectory. There was a narrow bed, an upright chair, a desk, and a small cupboard. There was no fire, and the room was icy.

"What is your name, Father?" Michael asked the curate.

"Father William Murphy," he answered.

"Well, from now on, you call me Michael. If you do not mind, I will call you William," he said, shaking the cleric's hand warmly.

William Murphy smiled. They were off to a good start, and the older man instantly liked Michael.

"Let us get the fires burning in these rooms, shall we? Nobody said we need to freeze to reach heaven."

William laughed.

"Father O'Connor was frugal, so we only lit the fires after five o'clock."

"I believe he—err—died?" Michael noted.

"Yes—of pneumonia."

"Well, there we go, William. There is a price for stupidity. We will keep the home fires burning, and anybody who needs warmth is welcome to be with us."

"We have twelve nuns next door in the convent, do the same rules apply?" asked William.

"Of course."

"Where do we eat?"

"At the convent. They have a small dining room next to the kitchen. You, and I eat there with the Mother Superior, and the rest eat in the kitchen."

"Should we set the cat among the pigeons, William?" Michael asked the curate.

William frowned.

"What are you thinking of doing?"

"From now on, we will all eat together in the kitchen. It'll feel like a family. I'll wager a bet with you that it'll be warmer and happier than the gloomy dining room."

William laughed out loud, this was going to cause an uproar, but it was time that the convent and the church moved out of the dark ages. William wondered what new ideas Michael would think of for the congregation, if this was what he was planning for the nuns.

On Michael's first Sunday, he stood behind the pulpit and looked out over the tiny congregation. There was Father William, twelve nuns who sang like angels, and a Mother Superior in attendance. In Michael's eternally optimistic soul, he viewed it as a practice round for the following Sunday, when the church would be full.

He raised the subject about the low attendance over luncheon. At first, the nuns were reluctant to give their opinions. To Michael's surprise, however, Mother Superior nodded her head in agreement and told them to state their views. It was their first experience of liberation, but it didn't take a lot for them to reveal interesting facts about the parishioners.

By the end of lunch, they'd identified several reasons for the low attendance. Some folk had to walk miles to reach the church. Many were old and ill. There were the usual sinners who believed that they were damned already. Of all the regular social issues in abundance, it seemed the Bunratty congregation was too drunk to get out of bed on a Sunday morning. Michael had to smile when Sister Colleen told them about a running feud between two families. The O'Learys would not allow the Mulroney family to cross their land. Cutting over the O'Leary farm shortened the Mulroney's trip to church to two miles, instead of seven. As far as Mr Mulroney was concerned, this was too far to travel for mere salvation and eternal life.

Michael returned to his room after lunch. The archbishop had been wrong, the small scattered Parish of Bunratty didn't need a minister, it required a politician. No amount of faith would solve these problems. It required an authoritarian intermediary with strong negotiation skills.

Michael sat down at the kitchen table with the curate and Mother Superior.

> "I want to travel to the farms every week and visit the folks who are too poor to get to church," Michael said.

Mother Superior gave her opinion.

> "The bishop is not going to like that, Father."

> "But who will do confessions and morning mass?" asked William.

> "It seems we usually have a maximum of three people per morning," Michael answered, and the other two agreed.

"This is not a pious community," noted William. "The town is small and poor, and the farmers are worse off still. The Great Hunger tested their faith and disappointed them. Out here in the sticks, they'd no support from Dublin, which left a bitter taste in their mouths."

"I empathise with how they feel," lamented Michael remembering his own impoverished start in life.

"I will leave on a Monday morning and return on a Thursday," said Michael. "I believe that we can restore hope and faith if we reach out. I will offer the parishioners mass and the eucharist at their homes."

"And confessions?"

"Oh, yes, there is that, is there not? Bloody—"

"—language, Michael, please. This is a church," insisted Father William.

"Is the eucharist not only delivered at people's homes on special occasions, for example, death?" asked Mother Superior disapprovingly.

"I'd hardly call death a 'special' occasion, Mother. It's not a party."

Michael laughed out loud.

"This is a—radical—concept, Father O'Neil. priests usually visit their parishioners to request tithes and nothing more!" she retaliated.

"Yes, Mother, that must also cease. People use any excuse to stay away because they're pressured to contribute," said Michael.

"But how would we survive without these tithes?" questioned Mother Superior.

"Mother, the lion's share of the money goes to Dublin, and not into the church buildings or priests. All money leads to all that glitters in Rome. All the money we get from our rich families to buy pews away from the poor goes straight to the Vatican."

Mother Superior and the curate both winced in horror.

"Don't let that kind of talk get beyond these walls, Michael. You'll be in a lot of trouble," warned William.

Mother Superior nodded.

"It's dangerous to talk indeed, William, but perhaps we need to show that we care. These peasants live in the most horrid conditions. If Michael can improve their lives, the authorities will surely show some compassion."

"Perhaps," William mused. "Food is scarce and the winter is harsh on them. Some of those little cottages have no flagstones, only mud floors, and the fuel is meagre."

"I still believe that if the people cannot reach the church, the church will reach them," insisted Michael.

"It's worth a small-scale trial if nothing else, I suppose. We might be able to keep it under wraps." said William.

"I doubt that. People talk. What will the archbishop say about it?" quizzed Mother Superior.

"I am likely to get a grilling," Michael answered matter of fact. "I will deal with that when he visits. I was told to take responsibility for our parish, and I cannot think of a better way than getting know them personally. We need to find practical rather than spiritual solutions for our lapsing flock. Kindness is the only way of winning their trust."

William's eyes widened. He'd never heard these radical opinions from anyone before. *Pandering to a sinful congregation? The next generation of priests are keen to do things differently from the old ways, it seems.*

"We are not here to wield power over poor people. We are here to offer them a reprieve when things become difficult—unbearable—for them."

At the best of times, Michael's ideas were controversial. Even-though everyone knew the bishop didn't expect a quiet life when it came to Father O'Neil's appointment, this radical outreach ruse would make him go berserk.

"Mmm, then there is still the matter of daily confessions to address," muttered William.

"That will be your job for three days of the week, William."

"Oh, Michael, must I? I have enough work keeping this place on the go by myself. Besides, I hate listening to confessions."

"William, you are a priest. I have every ounce of faith in you. Contrary to what the church says, let us use confession to lift these people off their knees and onto their feet, or we have served no purpose."

Mother Superior looked at William, who was grimacing. Michael's comment certainly gave new meaning to the effort required to 'raise people up.'

3

THE FEUD BETWEEN FAMILIES

Father Michael O'Neil spent his first two days on the road riding from hovel to hovel. He was sheltering from the constant rain, covered head-to-toe in oilskins. His progress was slow because, at every turn, the heavy wagon got bogged down in the mud. The going was rough. The cold exacerbated the misery, yet Michael was committed to keeping his end of the bargain and serving his parish.

The living conditions in the little thatched stone cottages were appalling. Michael had seen animals live in better conditions than these people. Their challenges during the winter were starvation, cold, and disease. Even on that first visit, he got a first-hand appreciation of his parishioners suffering. They lived in squalor. Shoeless children relied on ragged clothes to keep themselves warm. Families sat huddled cheek-and-jowl about small fires to make their dwindling wood and peat reserves last the winter. Water had to be fetched from a well, and the privy was a basic pit hole with a rickety wooden structure over it. At night they'd to go outside to perform their ablutions. After, they would return to share a bed with their parents and siblings who slept on worn-out mattresses made of hay.

Michael scrutinised their circumstances, and instead of demanding tithes, he asked Father William to supply them food.

> "Fill the wagon with whatever spare food we have squirrelled away here, and I will take it to them."

Father William muttered a string of profanities under his breath as did has he was told. *Who knows where next week's batch of 'generosity' will come from? Surely Michael knows this is all we have?*

A parishioner could see a wagon approaching. When he realised that it was a priest, he dashed to put the kettle on the fire so that the holy man could drink his 'welcoming' tea—and leave as quickly as he'd arrived.

> "Now, ye tell me, father," said Sydney McNamara, "how did ye get appointed to a godforsaken piece of The Emerald Isle like this? Us people have never yet had a priest in our house. Them previous ones were far too grand for the likes of us."
>
> "To tell you the truth, sir, the archbishop did not know what to do with me," chuckled Michael.

"So, he sent me to the first available—and far-flung—job he could find, presumably to keep me out of mischief."

The man didn't know if his unexpected visitor was telling the truth or pulling his leg.

"Take the weight off ye legs," said Sydney, pointing to a chair. "I am not calling ye 'father'. You got that, lad? Yer barely old enough to be me bloomin' grandson! What is yer name then?"

"Michael. Michael O'Neil."

"From around here are yer?"

"No, sir—from Galway side."

Maeve McNamara took out her best two cups and poured tea for Michael.

"Thank you," he said, smiling as he reached out for the warming brew.

"Sydney, get your boys to take a bag of flour out of that wagon, please. It's a gift in exchange for this wonderful tea," advised Michael.

Puzzled, Sydney and Maeve looked at each other. Then, the bemused wife nodded her head at Michael with a smile as she called for her boys.

Their sons carried in the big bag of flour. It was a pity the cleric didn't know that the family had just one week left of their winter rations, and the gift was his first miracle.

Michael finished his tea and offered to pray for the couple.

> "Oh, hell, Michael, I haven't got time for that. To tell you the truth, I got a yoke out there that needs fixin', no amount of bleedin' praying is gonna get that done."

Cheekily, the man added a request.

> "Come with me. Yer a strong lad yer are. We'll soon sort it."

Michael removed his cassock and gave it to Maeve for safekeeping. He spent a significant part of the afternoon in the barn fixing the axle on Sydney's old cart. The man was taken aback by the young priest's mechanical skills. When Michael had finished the job, the axle was as good as new.

> "Ye sure know about getting yer hands dirty," Sydney laughed. "I'm dying of drooth, lad, come in for some ale."

It was becoming dark outside.

> "Stay for the night, lad, will yer? There ain't no inn between here and the next farm."

Michael accepted. He slept on the dirt floor in front of their fire, and when he left, he paid them for his bed and board. It was the first time Sydney and Maeve had ever met an any man—let alone a churchman—who was so happy to pay for his lodgings.

"No, me boy! We dunna want the money. Ye helped me fine yesterday."

"You cannot eat an axle, Sydney. Accept payment, or I will never stay here again."

He blessed them, and they thanked him. Michael found himself riding away with a smile. I *have made new friends, and they'll surely look forward to seeing me again.*

Most of the small tenant farmers were the same—generous, funny, and grateful. A lot of them asked him to do small favours for them, like pay a bill or deliver a letter. They fed him whatever they were eating, and in the evenings, he was offered accommodation by a grateful parishioner.

When Michael later relayed the stories to William, he could not find the words to explain the joy he'd witnessed when they'd received the food. It was not only a gift—it was a lifeline.

Word travelled quickly, and soon everybody in the district knew that Michael was an excellent engineer. The men looked forward to his weekly visits. There was something tangible to discuss, instead of an awkward silence around the table while they waited for the priest to demand a tithe. Usually, if the parishioner could not afford their dues, the priest would mention that they would go to hell if it were not soon forthcoming. Many times, the churchman left with livestock that the poor tenant could ill afford to give away. There were also stories of priests being thrown out of the cottages and told never to return on pain of death. But Michael was not their priest—he was their trusted, compassionate, helpful friend. It was the first time they'd met a priest who practised what he preached.

Michael reached the Mulroney land and approached the large grey manor set in a perfect emerald green lawn. He counted twenty-four children taking advantage of a quick burst of sunshine to play in the garden, and he was impressed. It was a big family even by Roman Catholic standards.

He went to the front door and knocked. A nervous-looking maid opened the door. Inside were a large group of adults sitting in the parlour.

> "Father, we are not expecting you," cried Mrs Mulroney, flustered. "Oh my! Oh, do come in. Will you join my family in the parlour?"

Michael smiled.

> "Please do not feel uncomfortable. Mrs Mulroney, I have surprised everybody with my visits in the district."

Mrs Mulroney explained that her grandchildren were outside and that the adults around the table were her children. Everybody was charming, but reserved, and on their best behaviour. The manor was immaculate, but there was an underlying tension that Michael could not put his finger on until Shamus Mulroney arrived. As soon as Michael lay eyes on him, he realised that Shamus was a little tyrant.

Like a king at court, Shamus introduced himself and shook Michael's hand. As the family listened, the two men spent some time discussing the weather and the farm. Alas, neither Shamus nor Michael were good at small talk without any rapport between them, and soon they'd run out of conversation.

Shamus eventually broke the ice.

> "I suppose you want to know why you never see us in church, Father?"
>
> "No, not at all, I have come by to greet you and drop off some flour that we are distributing to the poor."
>
> "So, now the church thinks I am poor," sniggered Shamus? "Look about you, Father, do we look poor? I don't need your charity, man."

Michael sighed quietly. It had been a long day. The cleric was tired and didn't have the stomach for Shamus Mulroney's argumentative personality. Michael watched Mrs Mulroney becoming increasingly agitated. She'd have seen Shamus like this many times.

> "Not at all, but you have servants, and they have families. Perhaps you can take a bag for each of them."

Shamus nodded, looking down his nose. Michael studied him.

> "If you want to know why I am not at church, ask that oaf O'Leary next door."

"Sir, this is a friendly visit to introduce myself, not a summons to attend the Sunday service."

"O'Leary sits on land that has a road through it. Everybody in the area is allowed to use that road except my family—and I do not think your church is important enough to travel so many extra miles on a Sunday to go round the perimeter."

"Shamus, I have heard about the feud. Let us see? Perhaps the O'Learys will be reasonably when I talk to them."

"Do not ye give me that feckin' lecture boy. Every member of the church has promised a solution. What is so special about you then, now tell me?" shamus Mulroney ranted. "Besides, I do not want to touch that soil. I forbid my family near it. Even if he opened it to us, I would refuse to use it."

Michael found himself becoming increasingly irritated as Mr Mulroney became more insulting. It was clear that he was playing to the gallery, and his family was embarrassed on his behalf.

"Why not admit it, Father, yer only here for the silver coins, yer are!"

"My name is Michael O'Neil, and I am not a debt collector, Mr Mulroney," Michael said fiercely. "I am here to help the parish, not bleed it dry."

Shamus didn't know what to say next. He hadn't expected an objection from the young priest. Rather, he'd expected him to skulk off with his tail between his legs.

"I suppose the next thing you will want is my confession and then to pray for my absolution," shouted Shamus.

"No, sir, you can make your confession directly to God. I do not wish to represent you. At this moment, I would be a hypocrite if I prayed for you."

Shamus' jaw dropped. His children were accustomed to his abuse, and they never cheeked him. They looked on agog.

Shamus stormed out of the parlour and slammed the heavy door behind him. The remaining Mulroney family felt ashamed and tried to rectify their father's rudeness by being over-friendly. There was nothing that Michael could do to ease the tension that Shamus had caused.

Dylan Mulroney, Shamus' eldest son came over to him.

"I apologise on behalf of my father," he said.

"I hope that we see each other again under better circumstances," reassured Michael.

"Do you think you can get O'Leary to open that road for us? My mother would love to go to church on Sundays, so would my wife and children."

Michael frowned at the conundrum then quickly relaxed his face.

"I will do the best I can to help," he said, with a weak smile.

"Thank you," Dylan replied.

He greeted Mrs Mulroney and thanked her for the tea and the conversation. The priest hoped to see them again—but not soon.

Michael was filled with rage, and he could only hope that his anger would simmer down before he got to the O'Leary's home. If he'd to tolerate two ungrateful curmudgeons in a row. It'd be a tremendous drain on his appetite to help them.

Trying to make the best of the trying situation, Michael reprimanded himself for his uncharitable language.

4

THE FIRST DAY OF LOVE

Michael was still seething from the Shamus incident and had to take a few deep breaths before he was calm enough to knock at the O'Leary's imposing front door. A cheerful maid opened the ornate entrance, and she offered to call Miss O'Leary, as the master was not at home.

Michael stood in the entrance hall of the grand manor house and looked around him. It was far less stately than the Mulroney country pile, yet it felt inviting. The dogs lay in front of the warm fireplace. The furniture appeared faded, and books were strewn around the room. A warm blanket lay on the settee, while a pot of tea and teacups sat on the table. He could see the steam rising from the spout.

Michael was still taking in the scene when he heard her voice behind him.

"Good afternoon, Father. How may I help you?"

He spun around in surprise and looked into eyes that were so bright that it took a while before he could concentrate on the rest of her. The young woman was of medium height. A bush of wild hair accompanied her elegant features, and her skin was creamy and flawless. She was wearing a bright dark paisley skirt, and she was wrapped up in a brash bright purple shawl. Nothing that she wore epitomised period fashion. Her wild bohemian style screamed freedom, and if she wore black jewellery, she would easily have been mistaken for a gypsy.

"Good afternoon," he greeted her. "I am the new priest for the district, Father Michael O'Neil but please call me Michael, I do not enjoy titles."

The creature before him was disarming, and he could not remember feeling this way in front of anybody. She radiated confidence and seemed fearless.

She took in his appearance. He would've been described as black Irish by his fellow countrymen, with dark skin, pitch-black hair, and black eyes. He was tall, over six feet, with the body of a well-built farmer, a man not ashamed to do physical labour. He was more masculine than the other priests and ministers that she'd met before. His gaze was bright and cheery. He exuded positive energy. She'd a suspicion that he also came with a good sense of humour.

"My name is Justine O'Leary," she smiled. "—
And we are not Catholics."

All the anger that Michael was feeling dissipated, and he chuckled.

She observed that his laugh was expressive and spontaneous with none of the awkward politeness of his former colleagues. It suggested sincere delight.

"Come inside, please join me for tea."

"You're happy to have tea alone with me?"

"We are not alone. My mother is ill in bed, and my father will return soon. Besides, you come with boundaries."

Michael hoped he was not blushing. The subtle remark was a tad off colour, but it amused him that she was bold enough to say it. It was evident that Justine didn't have boundaries, and he found it remarkably provocative. He sank into a comfortable plush upholstered chair, grateful to be off the cart's hard bench seat.

Justine poured a cup of tea and put it on a mismatched saucer. Other families took out their best crockery when he arrived, and the lack of ceremony added to his relaxed sense of wellbeing.

"I suppose you are here about the Mulroneys," Justine said with an interrogating tone.

Michael sighed.

"I hope that I am not that predictable?"

"Did you meet Shamus Mulroney?" she asked.

"Yes, I did. He is exhausting."

Michael didn't know why he'd disclosed that information. It was far from ethical to do so.

"All I can tell you is that Papa will not allow him to put a foot on this land. My brothers have orders to shoot any Mulroneys on sight."

"You're surely joking?" he asked with a faint smile.

"Michael, I do not joke. You can take it up with my father. In fact, he has instructed my four brothers to show no mercy."

Michael noted that, as requested, she omitted his title when she spoke.

"Mmm, perhaps a little less murder may keep you all out of jail. I would hate to escort you all to the gallows."

Justine laughed loudly.

"Yes, maybe I am exaggerating a little, but Shamus has tormented our family for years."

"I can imagine that he would could feud forever."

"I will not have to tolerate him much longer, as I am moving to the village."

"Why is that? This farm is a beautiful place."

"Indeed, it is. But I am getting married," she said without emotion.

"Congratulations or sympathies?"

Justine picked up on the priest's sense of humour and laughed.

"I am not sure yet."

"Is he from this area?"

"No, he is from England. He is a vicar. Reverend Smithers. I do not know how he became employed by The Church of Ireland. They must have been short-staffed."

Michael chuckled.

"Mmm! Not every Protestant minister wants to live in these remote, staunch Catholic boroughs. Those poor men. When they're married, a vicar has to please his parish, his master, and his wife. That's why we Catholics have cut all that out and devote ourselves to the pope—I mean the Lord," he explained with a chuckle.

"Are you happy to leave? I cannot imagine you a minister's wife," Michael said, honestly.

"Neither did I," she replied, somewhat more severe now.

"You're likely to be his most difficult parishioner. I imagine your lively opinions can be—controversial."

"I hope to continue doing what I love when I live there. Perhaps I can open a small handicraft concern to uplift the local women," she added, smiling excitedly. "Besides, I am not going too far. I'm only moving to Bunratty."

"Uplifting local women? That is a progressive idea," said Michael, pleased they shared a common value.

"Indeed. Do you know that cottage industries are highly successful in France? The Industrial Revolution has impoverished many people, but artists, cabinet makers, and many others with particular artistic skills have created a market for rare and beautiful items."

Michael didn't know, and he was impressed with Justine's knowledge.

"Does your fiancé enjoy your art?"

"He tolerates it."

She frowned for the first time that afternoon.

"Do you ever sell what you make?" he asked with sincere interest.

"Only to Europeans. The British are not brave enough to invest in me. Their comments range from spiteful to unduly aggressive. Of course, it's even worse because I am a woman."

She smiled at him.

"Would you like to see the work I do?" she asked excitedly.

"I would love to," confessed Michael.

They walked across the courtyard to a whitewashed barn with a thatched roof. Justine opened the large door and led him inside.

"My father was going to knock it down—then he changed his mind and said I could use it."

The area was filled with items that only Justine could identify. Michael thought that he would find a neat little corner with soft brushes and pictures painted in delicate watercolours, but he was wrong. Not only did Justine have paintings lining the walls, but she also had sculptures. Clay, wood presses, hammers and anvils, an array of tools filled the barn. Every picture was a riot of colour. Yet for all its chaos, it reflected scenes that were recognisable but not in the traditional sense. He walked from item to item wholly absorbed by what he saw. It was bold and modern, and, even-though it was unorthodox, it drew in the viewer, absorbed them.

"I love it," stated Michael enthusiastically.

"Honestly?"

Her eyes lit up.

"Yes, it's an absolute reflection of your artistic nature."

"Nobody has ever said that to me before."

Michael just smiled and looked into her eyes. Eventually, he gazed back at the collection.

"It's perfect."

The bohemian moment made the young priest realise he'd spent so many years of his life working and studying at the behest of the brothers. He'd had no time to consider love, women, or even the dream of a family. His own life had been mapped out by others—a consequence of his early impoverished circumstances. He evolved into the priesthood. It had not been his conscious decision.

Michael stood looking at the art and watched her speaking. She was passionate, opinionated, and unapologetic. She was not the kind of wife that a clergyman was looking for. Instinctively, he knew that her marriage to the vicar was going to be a disaster.

He felt attracted to her in a manner that he'd never experienced before. Of course, Michael was male, and he'd sexual desires like all other men. He was capable of appreciating a beautiful woman and fantasising about her. Because of his training in the past, he felt he would've to repent afterwards on some level. Lately, however, he'd been prone to give up and accept his carnal desire for what it was—being a man of flesh and blood.

Michael looked at her and could see the curve of her bosom under her shirt and found himself becoming aroused. As he felt himself responding to her physically, he became aware that this was different. This was not simply a basic biological desire. An emotion accompanied it that he felt in his chest and his very soul. It was a combination of physical longing and loneliness.

Justine called him to look at a sculpture she'd started and explained how she engineered the bronzing process. He leaned over it as she showed him the details. He asked her questions and made suggestions, which she gleefully accepted. Knowledgeable and skilled, she answered his questions, comfortably explaining the technical intricacies.

Everything about Justine was sensual. The way she moved, spoke, even her clay-covered artistic hands. Her face was close to his. She turned to smile at him as she spoke.

Instinctively, and unexpectedly, he shocked himself by taking her face in his hands and kissing her. There was such overwhelming desire that they both gasped when they finally parted, shocked by what had just happened. For the first time that afternoon, Justine was speechless. He drew away from her abruptly.

"I am sorry," he said, boldly, sincerely and without shame.

Justine registered no remorse and smiled joyously back.

"I am glad that you have visited me," she whispered.

"Really?"

"Yes, very."

Michael kissed her again, and this time she responded. His hands moved over her body, touching her chest then moving down her back. Nothing that he'd fantasised about had prepared him for this. Somehow, it was purely instinctive—and he liked it.

She pushed her hand up under his shirt, feeling the hair on his body and his smooth muscular back. She pressed herself against him, pulling his head down to kiss her every time he wanted to pull away. He pulled up her skirt, touching her long bare legs.

As abruptly as they'd embarked on the journey, they both stopped. It seemed that they'd simultaneously had the same thought. *This all too much. Too soon. Too—!* Michael stepped away from her. They were both breathless.

"Stop. Not like this, Justine."

"Why not?" she whispered.

"This is all very sudden. I have never been with a woman," he confessed.

"Nor me with a man," she reassured.

"Are you afraid?" he asked her.

"No."

"Why now?"

"I do not love my fiancé. I may have known you but for a short moment, and I am afraid that I will never feel this way about any man again. The only time I have is now."

"I feel the attraction too," he whispered.

"Come with me," she urged, taking his hand land leading him upstairs in the little outbuilding.

There was nothing in the attic, and the floors were bare. They undressed, and Michael lay his cassock on the floor for her to recline on. He was overwhelmed by the beauty of her nakedness. They were not frightened, and they were not remorseful. They made love slowly, taking their time, secure in the knowledge that they were all alone. It was a sensational experience for both of them, and they felt an unshakeable, unbreakable love. Michael suspected that his 'convenient and practical' relationship with the church was over. It was only a matter of time before he would need to leave. He wondered what Justine felt and what she might do about Paul. He hadn't had the courage to ask her before he left.

Thankfully, it was a long ride back to the abbey, and Michael had plenty of time to live and relive their time together. He felt no guilt. She was engaged to marry another man, but that didn't concern him. His feelings felt intense and natural. The only thing that troubled him was that the experience had surpassed the physical. He felt an overwhelming connection to a woman whom he'd just met, and he wanted to keep her forever—despite the impossibilities.

Justine's mother observed her closely. Since the priest had visited, she seemed pensive and engrossed in her thoughts. Rosemary was anxious that Michael was introducing her to Catholicism. *What if he was successfully converting her?* Rosemary summoned her daughter. She seldom interfered in Justine's unique lifestyle and tried to be as gentle as possible with her wild child.

"My darling," began Rosemary, "you have been so distracted of late. Is there something wrong?"

"Not at all, mama," Justine said with a polite laugh.

"I have observed you, since that priest visited. You're not yourself. Is he trying to convert you?"

"Not at all, Mother. We did not speak about religion. I showed him my art."

"Was he shocked? Was he critical?"

"Not at all, he was very interested in what I did, and he complimented me on my work."

"Well, then, what is it, Justine? Why are you so flighty and distracted? I demand to know," rosemary asked firmly.

"Oh Mother," replied Justine, trying to hide the irritation in her voice. "I think that I have pre-wedding nerves. All very normal for a bride-to-be, wouldn't you say?"

It was not a complete lie. Justine's mind was in a turmoil. She'd no passion for Paul. She never believed that this depth of emotion she felt with Michael could exist. Because she let her lust consume her, she'd lost her virginity to a priest—a man whom she could never marry, engaged or not. *How am I going to survive my wedding night when my husband realises he was not the first man to have relations with me.*

5

LONELINESS AND DISCONTENT

For the first time in Michael's life in the church, he became restless and irritated. The price for comfortable certainty and convenience felt suffocatingly high. He felt trapped, stuck in a lonely world of tragedy. There was little joy except for weddings and christenings. The rest of his duties revolved around politics, social work and motivating unwilling people to be better versions of themselves.

Confessional sessions were of considerable irritation to him. Michael tried to field the responsibility to the curate as often as he could, thankful that for three days of the week, he didn't have to sit in the 'gossip box' as he dubbed it. He didn't know how much longer he could listen to Mrs O'Reilly repenting about her evil thoughts toward her sister, or Mrs Campbell making eyes at the postman. He knew that the local brothel and pub thrived, but he'd met very few men repenting for their promiscuous behaviour. Guilt, he concluded, was exclusive to women.

Michael couldn't discuss his discontent with William, as he didn't want to sow doubt in the curate's mind. Michael was not having a crisis of faith. He'd simply realised that he wanted to work, have a home, a wife, and a family and the two were mutually exclusive. Michael would always support the church's efforts to help the poor and needy, but on a personal level, he felt empty. *Even Adam had become lonely, and God had given him a partner, why not the same for me?*

Life in the parish continued, and to everybody's joy and relief, people began attending mass again. Slowly, but surely, the church became the centre of the town's activity. The 'unorthodox' priest had solved most of the broad issues in the parish, but the feud between the O'Learys and the Mulroneys continued to rage on.

Michael learned that as a leader he had strengths and weaknesses. He could motivate the congregation, but he refused to exploit them. Although the church coffers were empty, he refused to preach about tithes or collect them.

Once more, a little later in the day this time, he followed his route amongst his flock. This time, he didn't take the wagon, but rode on horseback. It was a refreshing trip with him seldom needing to dig the cart out of the mud. Again, his journey took him to his poor parishioners, where he brought them news, a role part-postman and part-priest. As the sun began to set late in the wintery afternoon, he rode past the imposing Mulroney Manor.

Michael knew that he was playing into Shamus Mulroney's hands by avoiding the family. He consoled himself with the excuse that he first had to speak to O'Leary. A visit to his manor would be most welcome. Secretly, the young priest was anxious to see Justine again. He was distracted, and every time his eyes closed, he saw her naked.

For the second time, a determined Father O'Neil knocked on the O'Leary's front door.

Douglas Edward O'Leary was impressed with the priest's firm handshake and confidence. He showed Michael into the study.

O'Leary was a large, well-built man with snow-white hair. He looked as strong as any forty-year-old, although he was in his sixties. Douglas could be intimidating amongst others in his class. He and was infamous in the district as a straight-talking farmer with deep empathy for his tenants, a quality lacking in most wealthy men.

"Can I pour you something, Father?" he asked the priest.

"Michael."

"I beg your pardon?"

"Call me, Michael. I find it difficult relating to people with all these titles between us."

O'Leary smiled.

"Have you come here to convert me?" O'Leary laughed, giving Michael a glass of Ireland's finest whiskey.

"Not at all, but I do need your help."

"With that little weasel next door, Mulroney?"

O'Leary seemed to be getting a tad hot under the collar thinking about his rancorous neighbour. Michael frowned and nodded.

"So, what happened between the two families, then" asked Michael.

"It was many years ago, about forty or more."

"You have been feuding for over forty years?" asked, Michael, amazed.

"I was courting my fiancée, and Mulroney took a fancy to her. She was lovely."

"Yes?"

"Well, he tried to convince her to cancel our engagement. One day, he arrived at her parent's manor house. I was visiting Rosemary. Shamus is no gentleman, let me tell you. We fought, right there in the parlour. We battered each other for quite a while. It was so bad we spent months paying off the damage that we caused. But Shamus was a bad loser. To be true, Michael, Shamus is a miserable little sod, so he is."

Michael tried not to smile.

"So, who won the lady?"

"I did, of course!" he laughed in delight. "Rosemary, and I have been married for thirty years—and she's still lovely."

Michael's thoughts returned to the beautiful Justine once more, and he was sure that O'Leary was right.

"I have an idea," suggested Michael, "it's somewhat unconventional, but I think it could pour oil on troubled waters. Why not play a game of football against the Mulroney clan every Saturday afternoon? If they win, they can cross your land, but if they lose, they stay at home."

"Who will be the referee?"

"I will," Michael answered gleefully. "I need to get some exercise."

"You?" exclaimed O'Leary, a broad smile beginning to develop.

"Good idea, boy. I will gather my team, and we will show the Mulroney mob who is in charge of this valley. We'll give them a long-overdue pummelling."

"But you need to be gracious if you lose, Sir."

O'Leary first frowned and then smiled.

"Ye gods, yes, I'm game for it, maybe get a boot in here and a fist in there."

With a deep sigh, Michael shook his head.

"Thank you, Douglas, I knew you would pull your weight."

"By the way, Michael, do you want to say hello to Justine? She's in her studio, tinkering with those blasted 'artworks' of hers. That girl has ideas of her own. I cannot get her out of there."

"Yes, please," said Michael hesitantly, aware that O'Leary was studying his reaction.

"I hope I wasn't being presumptuous, but I told the staff that you would be staying here for the night."

"Thanks for the offer, Douglas, but I must be off."

"I do not want to hear any objections. It's already dark and that horse needs to be fed—and so do you."

Michael nodded with reluctance, wondering how he would cope knowing Justine was within touching distance once more.

O'Leary took his visitor through the stable yard and to the outbuilding. Michael could hear a lot of blacksmithing noises coming from within it. He was surprised to see Justine wielding a massive hammer and beating the life out of a piece of steel on a hefty looking anvil.

"I'll leave you be, Michael, I have animals to tend to," said Douglas.

"You could not stay away, could you?" Justine purred.

"What are you busy with?"

"Come and have a look."

"You're far too comfortable with that hammer," he joked, pulling her gently toward him, and kissing her red-hot cheek.

"I missed you," he whispered in her ear.

Justine looked at him and smiled.

"I am glad."

She'd a fire going in the corner, and a small bellows was creating a blistering heat. Her perspiring face was flushed, and her dark tresses were sticking to her face. Justine was in the process of creating a sculpture that was currently unrecognisable, but she promised that It'd be beautiful when she'd finished it. He looked into her bright eyes and took in her smile. She was a happy soul, and it was contagious. Michael wondered if this is what all people would be like if they were allowed to work at what they enjoyed.

Michael watched Justine shaping the metal, then found himself becoming sombre. He'd that yearning again, the longing for a friend, a partner. But it couldn't be just anybody—it had to be her.

For the second time, he stepped toward her and pulled her into his arms. He kissed her, and he felt her body align with his. It was so natural, as if they were meant to be together, one life, one soul. He'd never been held or had a woman's affectionate touch since his mother died many years back. The sensation of touching and being touched by another human awed him.

Her energy flowed into him, and he choked with emotion. The last time he'd cried was when he watched his parents die on the side of the road. Blinking hard to crush the tears, he suppressed his feelings but held her close, absorbing her. She nuzzled her face against his neck and stroked his cheek adoringly.

"This cannot happen, Justine," Michael whispered.

"Because you are a priest?"

"Partly, but also because soon you are going to be married to somebody else."

"Can we not enjoy what we have at the moment? I do not want to think of the future when I am with you," coaxed Justine temptingly.

Dinner with the family was a jolly occasion, and because they were entertaining Father Michael O'Neil, all of the O'Leary siblings arrived, including their wives and children. Although it was an impromptu festivity,

Rosemary was a gracious hostess and made sure the priest received a warm welcome.

Michael saw why Douglas O'Leary had fallen in love with her. She was indeed beautiful. Clearly, Justine had inherited her sumptuous dark hair from her mother, although Rosemary's now had some silver starting to appear, which had lightened it. Although Justine was young and beautiful, her mother could still capture the attention of the room with her grace and stature. Rosemary was a woman that was cherished and cared for by her husband, and it was apparent in the way he looked at her. Her grandchildren flocked around her, waiting for their quota of attention. When she retired to the fireside settee for a moment of quiet and an aperitif before dinner, with great eagerness the youngsters clambered all over her, vying for her attention. She didn't chastise or shun them. It was evident they were adored by her.

"Get those bleeding little hooligans to be quiet
or I'll send them to bed with no supper,"
O'Leary roared at his sons.

None of them seemed to be perturbed by their father's instructions, and even their wives went about what they were doing without batting an eyelid at their father-in-law's exasperated expression.

At dinner, Michael was seated between Rosemary and an eleven-year-old little girl who didn't stop chattering. Douglas glared at her.

"The old dog is all bark and no bite," his wife whispered to Michael.

Justine caught Michael's eye several times during the meal and laughed as she watched him being challenged by her niece. The cleric took it in his stride. This was a happy family, not without their problems he supposed, but most definitely content. He coveted their lives, and he wanted the warmth of a family just like this—loving, loud, and unpredictable.

Justine's brothers were intrigued by Michael's engineering and farming knowledge. They spent a long time discussing new and advanced methods of farming, in particular the birth of steam tractors and ploughs which would expedite their planting methods and enable them to create larger fields and larger yields.

Afterwards, when they were alone discussing Michael, they agreed that he was quite a good fellow. They concluded it was a pity that he was a priest—he was wasted in his profession.

The family retired as Justine and Michael were still in deep conversation about some of her new artistic ideas. Contrary to convention, Douglas and Rosemary O'Leary excused themselves for the night and left their daughter to continue her conversation with the religious man, hoping his steadying influence would calm her wilder side. They were wrong.

Justine poured them each a whiskey, and they sipped it slowly as they sat looking into the fire, neither one speaking.

"Why did you become a priest?" Justine asked unexpectedly.

"Circumstances, I suppose. The Carmelite monks saved me from starvation during the Great Hunger. Out of necessity, White Abbey became my home. With the passing of my parents, they became my family."

"Have you ever wanted a woman?"

"Of course, I have—yes, even-though I am in the priesthood. What makes you think I am different from any other man of flesh and blood? But I think falling in love is different."

"What do you mean 'love is different'?"

Michael ignored her question and instead asked another one of his own.

"Why are you marrying Reverend Smithers?"

"There are few other options. It's either one of the few Protestant men from a local family or Paul Smithers. Unlike Shamus, the Mulroney brothers are good men, but my father would rather die than allow me to convert to Catholicism—and the Mulroneys are staunch. My father has no affection for Shamus Mulroney, and the wedding would be a bloodbath," Justine explained. "As you know, they were both in love with my mother, Rosemary. I think it's so romantic."

Justine's eyes twinkled and Michael laughed.

"Yes, I suppose it is—if you get to be with the girl you love."

She realised what she'd said earlier.

"I am sorry if I offended you with my question about love."

"Not at all. Matters of the heart visit us all at some time in our lives. Are you in love with Smithers?"

"Surely you appreciate women have so few options, Michael? Only the lucky marry for love. Paul, and I met some time ago," she explained. "I am twenty-six now, and I still live at home. Naturally, I chose not to 'escape' to a spinster's life of drudgery and poverty in domestic service," Justine shrugged before adding, "Besides, I will have children to keep me occupied."

"How do your parents feel about him?"

"I think my father only likes him for his religion, and my mother wants me to be financially cared for."

He looked at her silhouette in the firelight, and put out his hand to trace the shape of her body. In the late-night silence, the carriage clock on the mantlepiece struck midnight.

> "Come here," he whispered. "While we have a chance to be alone."

They undressed and stood naked in front of each other. It was a moment of great tenderness. She enthralled Michael. They'd made love to each other in the barn, but this time they were more comfortable in each other's arms, without first-time fears. Justine lay by the fire, and Michael lay next to her. They were less awkward as they lay entwined, engulfed by the escalation of intensity and desire.

Afterwards, they sneaked to their rooms, terrified of being caught. On the landing Michael whispered good night to Justine. They both knew it was more of a goodbye and the words were tinged with a heart-wrenching sadness that they would experience every time they thought of each other.

Michael was both surprised and relieved that Shamus agreed to the football matches, and soon the Saturday afternoon games became a source of entertainment for the whole parish. They played on the border of the two adjacent stretches of farmland, and people would delight in taking a walk over to watch the shenanigans.

During the first few matches, there was a lot of cursing and punching, but Michael laughed and took it in his stride. On these occasions, when play got out of hand, it was tempting for him to blow his whistle and stop play, to threaten the teams with the burning flames of hell itself if they didn't rein in the viciousness. However, that was not how Michael chose to deal with the on-pitch conflict. He made sure that he played the men so hard, that by the end of each match, they'd no aggression left in their bodies.

And this is how the ferocious O'Leary and Mulroney feud began to fade. The Parish of Bunratty was not yet Eden. Their corner of the world was still awaiting paradise, but at least the two bitter patriarchs stopped threatening each other with death. Although the older men would never be friends, their sons and daughters began to speak and rebuild the old bridges that their fathers had burnt. Week after week, Justine attended the matches, and the more the young priest saw her, the more he fell in love.

Eventually Douglas O'Leary relented, and the Mulroney family were allowed to pass through his land every Sunday and thanks to a much shorter journey, they attended church more regularly. The matches became an institution, and developed into a small district football club. Shamus Mulroney would always have a temper. He was a terrible loser, nevertheless every so often, Mulroney would slaughter a sheep and send the parcelled-up meat to the O'Leary family. It was his way of showing gratitude. The old fellow didn't know how to thank O'Leary for scaling back the hostilities, so he displayed his appreciation in the best way that he knew how—to send a gift.

Michael arrived at the O'Leary's house late on a Wednesday afternoon. Fiona, the young maid, opened the door. Instead, of being her usual cheerful self, she was serious.

"Please come in, Father Michael," she said.

"What is wrong, Fiona? You look as if something terrible has happened."

Fiona looked downcast.

"Reverend Smithers is in the parlour with Miss Justine. Let me announce you."

Fiona looked at the visitor with a concerned expression. Michael had been caught off guard. Unconsciously, his face scowled as he felt a jealous resentment course through him. The young maid had picked up on his mood.

She led him into the now-familiar parlour. Reverend Smithers and Justine O'Leary were sitting on a small settee nestled in a large bay window.

Justine and Smithers stood up to greet him. The room felt cold and formal. The easy-going atmosphere that he'd always enjoyed in the O'Leary home on previous visits had evaporated. He was sorry that Douglas was not there. A big character like his would've eased the quiet tension.

"Hello, Father Michael," greeted Justine with a forced smile. "Please meet Reverend Smithers."

Michael and Smithers shook hands with each other.

"My dear fellow, please call me Paul."

It was a day for which Michael had not prepared. He'd never anticipated facing Paul Smithers at the O'Leary home, a place which he'd increasingly come to consider his territory since taking over the parish.

"Father Michael, are you looking for my father?" asked Justine meekly.

Michael didn't recognise the curiously weak woman standing in front of him. It was like someone else had taken over her body.

"Yes, Miss. Is he here?"

"Do you mind seeing yourself through to his study?" Justine asked.

He nodded with secret resignation.

Michael knocked on Douglas O'Leary's study door.

"Hello, Michael!" roared Douglas. "Come and join me for some of Ireland's best," he said and began pouring two large glasses of whiskey before he got an answer.

"Did you meet Reverend Smithers? That chap my daughter is marrying?"

"Yes, I did."

"The only time in months that we attend a church service, and what happens? Paul Smithers starts courting Justine. God knows what she sees in the man."

Michael nodded but didn't offer any comment.

"You're joining us for dinner?" Douglas asked him.

Michael was hesitant. He looked out of the window. The rain was falling in torrents, and it was icy cold. He knew that it was unfair on his horse to travel in such bitter conditions, but he could not will himself to watch Justine with another man.

"You cannot be thinking of taking that poor animal out into the cold?" asked Douglas.

"You're right," Michael answered in resignation.

"Besides, I have been getting used to your midweek visits," confessed Douglas cheerily.

Justine and Paul Smithers sat beside each other at the dinner table, and Michael sat next to Rosemary. Michael tried focusing his attention on Douglas and Rosemary, but he couldn't help looking across the table and studying Justine. She was trying very hard to be normal. Perhaps she succeeded in convincing her fiancé—but she didn't convince Michael.

The priest guessed the man's age at about thirty. He was of medium height, had immaculately styled hair, clean-shaven smooth clear skin, piercing blue eyes and a strong, chiselled jawline. Paul Smithers, it seemed, was a very handsome fiancé indeed.

Paul opened the conversation.

"I believe that you have been quite successful in drawing people back to the Sunday services, Michael"

"Yes, we have a many more people in attendance now."

"I am pleased to hear that," Paul replied. "No, church can function without contributions and collection plate offerings from the parishioners. It puts the food on our table."

"Well," said Michael, "our coffers are empty."

Paul laughed.

"Surely not? Part of the Catholic Church impoverished? Quite inconceivable. You collect tithes every week, no?"

Michael bristled at the suggestion. *Typical! A career cleric with no concern for his congregation, only himself.*

"No, I deliver food to those in need on my weekly visits."

"Well, I never," said Paul in his sophisticated English accent. "I have never known a church to have that policy."

"It's not a church policy—it's my policy," said Michael with steel in his voice.

"I think it's a damned good idea, Father," roared Douglas O'Leary. "A wonderful demonstration of upholding good Christian values for the benefit of your flock, not just paying lip service to them in sermons from the pulpit."

Paul Smithers felt slighted at the comment, and the first gurgle of resentment was born.

"I am exhausted," announced Michael after dinner. "Douglas, Rosemary, will you please excuse me? I need to leave early tomorrow."

"Of course, my boy," said Douglas affectionately. "You know where your guest bedroom is. Put your head down and rest."

Paul felt another pang of resentment. His relationship with Douglas was polite at best. Seeing O'Leary be so genial to the priest made his chest tighten. He was furious.

In the early hours of the morning, Justine tapped lightly at Michael's door. Unable to sleep, pining for a future he could never have, he crept over and opened it. She pushed her way over the threshold without being invited, and tried to cling to him.

With uncharacteristic coldness, Michael removed her hands from his chest.

> "Go back to your room, Justine. This is not the time nor the place. You have spent the day with your fiancé discussing marriage plans."

Justine was confused by his defensive response. It was the first time that Michael had rejected her. Hurt, angry and bewildered, she left his room in silent shame.

Tip-toeing past Paul's room, she noticed she'd no desire whatsoever to knock on his door and fling herself into his arms.

6

THE CONFRONTATION

Justine and Paul Smithers were married for quite some months before Father Michael was finally forced into their company—the occasion the annual country fair. Michael stood next to a barrel of stout when he saw Paul Smithers walking toward the beer stall. He wanted to avoid the man, but they found themselves standing next to each other at the bar.

Michael greeted Paul good-naturedly and put out his hand.

"Hello, Father," said Smithers.

"Well, well, well. It must be years since we last met."

Paul gave a false smile.

"We never seem to have enough time to speak when we see each other in the village."

"Yes, it has been a long time," Michael said, feigning interest.

"Yes, I believe that you are still basking in the glory of solving the old parish feud," said Paul, as if nobody respected Michael before that.

Michael laughed to hide his resentment.

"Can you believe the amount of trouble a beautiful woman can cause?"

"Yes, I am married to one, remember? Luckily, with your vow of celibacy you will never have that problem," said Smithers, a slight smile developing at the corners of his mouth.

Michael took the barbed comment in good humour. *That was then, this is now. She's with him these days.*

"Sometimes, I wonder if that vow is a blessing or a curse," he responded, smiling broadly.

Reverend Smithers put his head to one side questioningly.

"Talking about beautiful women, who told you about Shamus coveting young Rosemary? That was years ago? Gossiping parish tongues wagging again, no doubt?"

"Oh, no—it was your father-in-law."

"Ah, yes, of course. Douglas was quite fond of you, was he not?" Paul asked sarcastically.

"Indeed, he was—and still is. To this day, we play football on his land every Saturday."

"Do you know that my wife Justine, and I have been wedded for over two years now? How time files," reverend Smithers added.

"Yes, I believe so," replied Michael confidently, followed by a mutter of "That is more time than I would've given the marriage."

Smithers glared him.

"From what I remember, your wife is lovely. You're a fortunate man."

Paul nodded uneasily, uncertain about how she'd felt about the dashing young priest. Michael was economical with the truth.

"Yes, I got to meet Justine before you were married. I was trying to get the Mulroneys to attend my Sunday services, so I visited Douglas O'Leary and had dinner with the family. Douglas insisted I stay, you see. They were very generous. Justine showed me her art. You must be very proud of her?"

Reverend Smithers didn't reply straight away but took a sip of his ale.

"All that art business of hers was a lot of nonsense. I put a stop to it when we got married. She's a minister's wife and her duty now is to serve the parish. Besides, she was atrocious at it. I told her I would not tolerate her embarrassing me with that amateurish rubbish."

The word 'tolerate' annoyed Michael. It made Reverend Paul Smithers appear more like a dictator than a devoted husband. *What sort of life is she having with him? It sounds like she's being kept like a prized caged bird.*

Michael saw Justine approaching. He was somewhat relieved that she didn't appear to have seen him. His head desperately wanted to excuse himself and skulk away quietly—but his heart riveted him to the spot.

The priest watched her dutifully take her husband's arm. Her smile wavered when she saw him. Justine Smithers had gone to extraordinary measures to avoid him when she moved into the little rectory in Bunratty village and had succeeded until now.

Michael studied her carefully. The captivating free spirit he'd met years ago was no longer free.

"Hello, Father," she greeted distractedly, so desperate to avoid Michael's gaze she pretended to wave to somebody in the crowd.

"—Good day, Mrs Smithers," he said after a nervous pause.

Michael looked directly into her eyes. In that moment, he remembered the delicious afternoon in the outbuilding and the passionate fireside evening as if it were yesterday. He'd lived and relived those times repeatedly, and he found himself becoming aroused as he thought of their brief encounters.

"Your husband, and I have met over a pint. We have agreed the ale is lovely. We have something else in common at last," Michael joked.

Michael had not meant the statement to be ambiguous, but she'd taken it up that way. Justine blushed and looked at Paul Smithers nervously. Michael had tried to make small talk but had chosen the wrong subject to break the ice.

"You must be missing your studio now that you have other responsibilit—"

"—I told him you do not do art anymore," Smithers interrupted.

"It was a practical decision. There is so little space in the rectory, and I am very busy these days. So, yes, unfortunately, I cannot unleash my creative side anymore. Still, other the challenges are equally satisfying."

"What a pity," Michael said. "You showed such promise. I suppose your idea to use traded handicrafts to lift up the disadvantaged women in the parish has come to nought too?"

Michael stared at her, mesmerised. She was so beautiful, but her eyes were not quite as bright as they used to be. Her luscious wavy dark hair was scraped off her face and twisted into a tight knot behind her head in an attempt to tame it.

Her plain yellowing straw hat was dreary, as was an equally drab grey dress. There was no vivid colour or any expression of her real self. Her husband had transformed her into a faded canvas. The delightful joyous freedom that she radiated was gone. Michael suddenly felt sad, like a part of him too had died. He wanted to keep her, protect her, bring her back to life. He longed to restore her to her former glory, back to the way she used to be that first time he saw her she tearing down the outbuilding steps, greeting him with her joyous, uncensored voice.

Justine excused herself and went off to assist a nearby stallholder selling cakes to raise money for the parish. Reverend Smithers stood silently smouldering.

"You seem to know a lot about my wife, Father."

"Only the little I learned on my visits to the estate."

"Stop discussing her art. That's all in the past," Paul warned coolly. "She's satisfied with her new life as my wife."

Michael nodded in resignation.

"I apologise if I seemed over-familiar with your wife."

"You flatter yourself. You're not a threat to my marriage, Father O'Neil. To all intents and purposes, you are nothing more than a eunuch," reverend Smithers censured with a polite smugness.

If Michael were a better person, he would've walked away instead of reacting to the snide remark. If he were a vengeful man, he would've told Paul Smithers there and then that he was the first man to bed his wife, not him. He held his tongue because he would never let his beloved Justine be caught in the crossfire between her two suitors. Equally, he was not going to let Smithers' inflammatory comment pass him by.

His black Irish temper got the better of him, and turning the other cheek was the last thing on his mind. Michael punched Paul Smithers with a force that sent him flying backward over the beer barrels. He landed on the emerald green grass in shock. A punch from a priest was the last thing that he'd expected.

Reverend Paul Smithers lifted both his hands toward his face and cupped his bloodied nose. Embarrassed, he remembered that he was still on the ground. Smithers was desperate to spring to his feet in a flash lest too many people witness his humiliation at the hands of Father O'Neil. Alas, before he could get up, the raging priest bent over his nemesis, grabbed him by the front of his shirt and dragged him to his feet.

"Please show me more respect in the future, Reverend."

The locals were delighted that Father O'Neil had walloped Smithers. They too felt smug selfishness was not an endearing quality and that the arrogant little git had it coming for some time. It just happened to be a priest who dealt the hammer blow.

If Michael knew what the consequences of his action would be, he would never have raised his mighty fist against the minister—because the cowardly Paul Smithers would make Justine pay for Michael's sins not him.

Later that day, back at the rectory Smithers struck Justine so violently that she flew over their marriage bed and landed in a heap on the other side. For a moment, she was too distracted by the lights flashing behind her eyes to respond emotionally. She'd heard of people seeing stars when they were struck against the head, but now she was experiencing it for herself.

As the impact of the blow registered in her mind, Justine sat herself up using the wall as a support. She put her hand up to her cheek, which felt like the bone was crushed. She could feel blood trickling from her nose, but she didn't flinch or cry. She was furious, and all that Paul Smithers saw was a pair of eyes boring into his with hatred.

> "Do you think that I am stupid, Justine? It's my job to study people. I have waited years to find out who the man was that deflowered you before your wedding night—and today I met the rascal."

Justine wanted to scream 'Yes, it was him,' desperate to take a step to be with the man she truly loved, but she could not betray Michael.

"That's ridiculous, Paul. He is a priest," she yelled.

"Do not make me do this to you again, Justine. I suggest you learn your lesson and stay away from Michael O'Neil," threatened the betrayed husband, in a cold callous voice.

Now, Justine was on her feet, tending to her wounds.

"My father will kill you if he knows what you have done to me."

She looked in the mirror. The large bruise on her face was already purple, and her closing eye lid was an angry swollen red.

"Your father and mother are in Ulster, and you will stay in this house until you look better. I will tell everyone that you are sick and not receiving visitors."

"I will not live with you another day."

"You're my wife, Justine, and as you promised in your vows, you will honour and obey me."

"Get out!" she screamed. "Get out and never come near me again."

Justine was overwhelmed with hatred for her brutal husband. It was instant and irreversible. She would never spend another night in his bed, and she would return to her father's house. She might be able to secure her own safety, but she could not guarantee her husbands. *The rotter will be lucky if Papa does not beat him to death for this attack.* The thought of her father finding out delighted her, and she stifled a vengeful smile.

"You can go straight to hell, Paul Smithers. I will never obey you," she yelled fearlessly.

Enraged by her defiance, he came storming towards her. He hit his wife with the back of his hand. Once more she went sprawling onto the ground. The blow was so forceful, his wedding ring split her cheek open, and blood ran down her face.

"You'll obey me, Justine, or there will be more where this came from. I do not care how long it takes, but I will break you until I have the wife that I want."

"You're a monster," she screamed.

"For better or for worse, Justine. If you defy me, it'll become worse."

Justine stood up for the second time, her hair had come loose, and it looked like surrounded her face like dark drab curtains. Paul Smithers failed to spot a small hint of a sparkle through the swollen purple flesh around her eyes.

Although in agony, Justine was calculating and astute. She noted he was standing in front of a heavy footstool by the dresser. She sprang towards him and pushed with all her might. Smithers lost his balance, fell back, and tripped over the stool. He landed on the floor for the second time that day.

Justine spun around in a graceful motion and grabbed the poker from the fireplace. She raised it high above her head, like a Celtic warrior. Justine knew that if she killed her husband she would hang, and so she did the next best thing she could think of. She brought the poker down on his knee cap. The brute screamed in pain as the blow landed. Instinctively, he tried to pull the injured leg up towards him to investigate the damage, but it was pointless. He could only scream in in agony. He lay on the floor, every floundering movement taking him to the cusp of unconsciousness. Justine brought the poker down upon his leg twice more, ensuring that the knee cap was irreparably shattered. Then she threw the weapon back into the fireplace.

She kneeled on the floor next to him and pushed her smashed, swollen, bloody face as close to his as she could stand to be.

"Tell your parishioners you fell off your horse, you filthy rotten sod," she hissed.

"I will find you, and you will be sorry!" Paul Smithers cried out.

"Every time you lean on your crutch, every time you feel agony tear through your body, remember how you beat me."

She spat in his face.

"You'll pay for this, Justine!"

"Till death we do part, Paul Smithers, and it shall be yours if you dare hurt me again."

She stormed out of the bedroom. As the door swung open, she was met by several eavesdropping servants' ears. Her staff looked at her with deep sympathy, appalled by what they saw and heard. Their sympathies lay with Justine not their odious master.

Although it took a lot of effort and great courage, she held her head high and walked defiantly to the stable where she saddled a horse. She covered herself against the cold and rain and rode back to her father's house.

7

THE CONFESSION

Michael walked to the church at Bunratty and found Father Murphy pottering around the building. It was something that priests did to alleviate boredom.

"Has the news reached your ears yet?" Michael asked.

"Of course, it's a small village," sighed William.

"Who told you?"

"A young girl was selling eggs at the fair to raise funds for the roof repairs. She gave the good news to Mother Superior, who came and told me."

"Does anybody else know?

"Of course, the whole parish knows by now, and it has probably reached Dublin," William Murphy answered, unimpressed with the young man's unruly and lascivious behaviour.

"I do not need a tongin' from you, William," Michael sighed.

"Catch yourself on lad. You've been away in yer head for the last while. You're a priest. Start acting like one."

Father William Murphy walked away and went into the confessional booth, raising a demanding eyebrow at his colleague before disappearing inside.

Michael felt way out of his depth. His life was spinning like a top, and he didn't know how to escape the vortex that was sucking him into the carnal lay world. He didn't know what had possessed him to behave like a hooligan. It was not a matter of if, but when the letter would arrive summoning him to the archbishop in Dublin demanding an explanation for his wayward and disreputable behaviour.

Michael opened the door to the confessional and sat down. William Murphy half opened the wooden shutter screen that separated them, waiting for Michael to begin his unburdening his soul.

"Father, forgive me, it has been a long time since my last confession," Michael muttered.

"Go ahead, my son," William said seriously.

"William," Michael hissed, "don't you dare let this story get further than this box, do you understand me?"

William rolled his eyes.

"You know that everything you say—"

"—Promise me," insisted Michael, not allowing William to complete his sentence.

"Yes, I promise."

"William, I want to leave the church," Michael blurted out.

The repentant priest heard a heavy sigh on the other side of the screen.

"How long have you felt this way?" William asked.

"A couple of years or more, just after—" Michael's voice trailed off.

"Why have you waited so long to talk about it? I am not empowered to help you with your decision. You should to seek help from a more qualified person than me."

"Of course, you are qualified."

"No, Michael, you should be discussing this with the bishop. Leaving the church is a grave matter."

"Has your quarrel with Paul Smithers got something to do with this crisis of faith?"

"Yes. I am in love with his wife."

"What?" exclaimed the curate.

"Stop making such a noise, William. If there is somebody in the church, they'll hear you."

"Well, I have to say I am shocked. Disappointed too."

"I fell in love with Justine O'Leary well before she married Smithers."

There was no reply from William.

"She's the only woman I want, the only woman that I have touched."

"Oh, heaven's above, Michael. This is all too much, boy! What was going through your mind? Being tempted by the sins of the flesh after all your good work in this parish!"

"I want a family with her. I want to experience true joy," Michael lamented, unsure he would ever have his wish granted.

He'd mourned Justine for two years, and he knew he would miss her every day, for the rest of his life. Things were becoming unbearable.

"Need I remind you that you are anointed and entrusted with other people's souls, Michael. You have a duty to God before anything else."

"Bloody hell, William," Michael snapped, "I do not want the responsibility of other people's souls. Looking after my own poses enough of a challenge."

"Calm down. And stop with that bad language! Now, are yer listening to me, you little thug? You have surely lost all yer marbles wanting to give up the priesthood," William chastised, annoyed by Michael's rebellious attitude.

Michael capitulated to his colleague's wishes and chose to listen to William's words of wisdom.

"And how did this happen, then?" William asked, salacious curiosity getting the better of him.

"She stood in front of me naked, and I fell in love with her."

"Lust, Michael," corrected William. "That was lust, sent directly from the devil. It's one of the seven deadly sins."

"Don't be so patronising. Even priests know what lust and desire are and that we have to avoid it, ignore it, or repent for it. This was different. I felt such a sense of longing, not just from my loins. I want a loving woman in my arms. I am tired of being alone."

"If this gets about the parish, we're going to be in a lot of trouble, Michael. Not one word about Justine Smithers must reach the ears of the nuns. They gossip like the best of 'em," advised the curate staring straight ahead, deep in thought. "Nor the bishop, or the archbishop. Agreed?"

The two men were starting to understand the gravity of the matter.

"Agreed!" confirmed Michael.

"The news of the brawl can—and will, no doubt—reach the archbishop's ears, but the girl must never be spoken of," William warned.

"You know, William, I did not choose my destiny. It was not a calling. As an orphan, it was chosen for me. I never met women, and they were not allowed in the monastery. We were warned of temptresses who would lead us astray. Every female was sent to seduce us like Medusa. But God created Eve because Adam needed a partner. Must I walk through this long, difficult life alone, denied the experience of womanly love?"

"You know what the bishop would say, do not you?"

"Of course, I know what his blasted answer would be. But surely falling in love cannot be a sin? Love is a beautiful human emotion that brings light to the world, nothing like the darkness that stalks murder or greed."

"You tell me, Michael. Look at what a state you are in, you've a jibbering wreck for days, man!" teased William with a grin. "Perhaps you should've confessed this sooner. A problem shared is a problem halve—"

"—I did not know if you would understand how I felt," interrupted an agitated Michael. "Does the church allow a priest to leave and follow a regular life?"

"Yes, they do," comforted William. "—Eventually. There will be a lot of questions, of course, but they also know that we clerics are humans."

"The thing is, even if I do leave the church, I doubt I will be happy. I'll never meet another woman as special as Justine. Why did she have to marry that awful brute of a man. Whether I leave or not, I can never bloody well be with her."

William sighed.

"What did I tell you about cursing in here?"

Michael apologised yet again.

"Have you ever been in love, William?"

"Yes, I have fallen in love many times."

"Why are you still in the church?"

"Fear, mostly. Fear that a woman would not want me. Fear of being physically inexperienced. Fear of going through the process of being laicised. Fear of what career to follow after I left."

His reply resonated with Michael. William had voiced all the fears that haunted him too.

"Look, lad, make yer choices now. You're still a young man, and you have those engineering skills to fall back on. In ten years, or so, you will be more comfortable, less confident, and have fewer opportunities. If you really want to go, go now," William guided gently.

"The bishop is going to be as mad as a box of frogs."

"I think that the bishop will be less surprised than you think. You have never followed the rules well," William mused.

"I am not rebelling against the church. I have been heartened by my ability and efforts to help those parishioners in need. If I could marry Justine and stay in the priesthood, I would. But I am full of guilt. If I choose her, does it mean that I love God less? Without the church taking me in, I am sure I would be dead by now. This is a complete mess."

William shook his head.

"The bishop will expect you to repent and spend time reflecting on your actions, and only then will he allow you to make a final decision. He will grant you a fair hearing. You have to remember that the last thing the church wants are errant lapsed priests running around tarnishing the name of the Catholic Church—there are enough of them already."

"To be honest, William, I do not feel repentant. I would do everything again. I would make love to Justine again, whether she is married to Paul Smithers or not."

"Make love? Jesus, Mary and Joseph," William groaned. "I thought you merely kissed the girl? What else have you left out?"

"We made love more than once."

"Now, I can understand why Paul Smithers is exasperated with you! What must he have thought on his wedding night when he discovered his lovely new wife was not 'intact?' Between you and I, I find that vile man getting his comeuppance rather amusing."

Lost in his own little world, Michael laughed out loud, feeling lighter for sharing his woes. William, however, fell silent for a while, searching for the right words to continue.

"I too have felt that aching loneliness and have regularly sought comfort throughout my career."

"Does that mean that you sought a woman's conversation?"

"No, it means that I had sex with prostitutes."

Michael was shocked by the cold admission.

"I, too, wanted to experience physical love."

"Were you filled with guilt?"

"In the beginning," William confided. "I suffered terribly from guilt and regret, the fear of being found out. However, as I became older, I realised women are a great comfort and men need them in their lives. It's unnatural, cruel even, for men to be alone from birth to death."

Michael became deadly serious again.

"This is all so confusing. The bible teaches us one way of living and then we want another. Some clerics are able to act on those womanly feelings. Others, like us, are forced to lead double lives, flooded with guilt. It's the guilt that I cannot deal with. Thank you for listening to me, William."

"Go in peace, son, and sin no more."

"What penance must I do?"

"A hundred utterances of the Lord's prayer are not going to help, my boy. If you're in love as much as you say you are. You'll need to be brave and make your own choices from here on. There are many ways to serve God, but you must be congruent. You must make your life choices accordingly, or you will never be at peace. If you want a woman and a family, have one and serve the Lord in your own way. You're of no benefit to anyone— or yourself—if you spend your life pretending to be someone whom you are not."

A letter arrived addressed directly to Michael. He was hesitant to open it, expecting to be summoned to Dublin. Although the letter was covered with stamps and seals, Michael convinced himself that the letter didn't look official enough to have come from the archbishop. Of course, he knew that he was fooling himself.

The document instructed him to present himself to the Archdiocese in Dublin within two weeks. The glacial Irish rural postal service meant he didn't have a lot of time left. Wanting to say goodbye to the parishioners who lived far afield, he packed his bag and planned to leave at first light.

For what he suspected would be the last parishioner visits in an official capacity, Father Michael O'Neil set out on a cold, rainy morning. He took the parish cab, put on oilskins against the weather, and ensured that he'd sufficient horse blankets for the mare.

The final visits to his flock were bittersweet. He'd a natural affinity to bond with the ordinary folk who had come to appreciate his skills. He loved helping them to build and fix things with his practical knowledge, delighting in improving the quality of their lives. His ideas and commitment to help were both limitless.

During the lean years, he'd raised money and food for those who were struggling. During the fat years, the farmers had repaid the industrial folk for their generosity. He would miss their kindness. They too had become part of his extended religious family, and in return, he'd become their benevolent son.

Shamus Mulroney shook Michael's hand. The old insults were long forgotten. Although Shamus would always be volatile, he'd softened somewhat over the years. For the first time in their marriage, Shamus told his wife that he loved her, and she no longer walked in the shadow of Rosemary O'Leary. Shamus appointed himself the head and referee of the small football club they'd started. It was the first time that he'd ever received praise for his social responsibility.

> "But you have to be fair, Shamus. You cannot lose your temper, or everybody will leave—the goodwill that we created will be destroyed. Carry on in the spirit we started, eh? I am sure you will do a good job if you set your mind to it," Michael lectured.

Shamus nodded eagerly, half in agreement, half with pride.

> "I am entrusting you with the job of keeping the peace throughout the parish."

As Michael left Shamus, he knew that his last stop would be the O'Leary manor. He'd thought of avoiding them and sending a letter. Still, if Michael visited everybody else and chose to exclude Douglas and Rosemary O'Leary, it'd be a grave insult. It'd also confirm suspicions about his past with Justine, depending on what the gossips had made of the evidence presented.

So, as difficult as it was, he arrived at their manor on a dark Friday afternoon.

"Father Michael, good day," greeted a cheery Fiona.

She was ever the friendly young woman, and he like to treated her with respect and kindness. Despite being low down in the pecking order, in his mind, she was as much a part of his congregation as anybody else was. Michael had discovered Fiona was forced to leave school early and go into service when her father died unexpectedly and her poor mother could not afford to feed her. He'd arranged that she learn to read with the local Sunday school teacher and improve her career prospects. She would be forever grateful for his generosity.

"How are you, Fiona?" he enquired.

"Very well, thank you, Father."

"Is Mr O'Leary at home?"

"No, Father, they have gone to visit family in Tipperary. They'll return on Sunday."

"Well, I hope you have the kettle on Fiona. I need something to warm me up before I leave."

"Miss Justine is here."

"I see," Michael said, his heart pounding.

"Do come in, Father. It's blowing a hooley on the doorstep. I shall call her for you."

At that news, Michael's heart did a somersault.

On hearing of his arrival, Justine came dashing down the stairs as Fiona went off to make the drinks. Justine had a thick scab from the cut on her cheek and her bruised face was a mixture of purple, blue and yellow. Her dark hair was wild, her clothes bohemian. One more, everything she wore was entirely out of fashion. Her eyes were bright, and her smile was broad. *She's back!* She rushed into his arms with joy.

Justine took the opportunity to kiss Michael passionately and unapologetically, not caring if, and when Fiona returned. He took her face in his hands, pushed her hair back, and examined her.

"How did this happen?" asked Michael.

"After the quarrel at the fair, he was furious."

"I will kill him. I swear to God that I will kill him," said Michael, raw emotion and fury in his voice.

He held her firmly to his comforting chest, stroking her hair.

"I am so sorry he hurt you."

"I do not want to talk about him, Michael."

"Are we alone," he asked.

"Yes, until Sunday," she answered.

"Where is your husband?"

"He is at the rectory."

Michael tilted his head to one side questioningly.

"He has a severe leg injury. No man will ever beat me. I am my father's child. You might here tittle-tattle in the village that he fell off his horse," she explained with a wicked triumphant smile.

Michael grinned at more signs her wild streak was back.

"Can you stay with me until Sunday, Michael? Please, can we spend this time together?"

"Why, Justine? Why do we want to torture ourselves again after all these years? Shouldn't we let bygones be bygones?"

"But we love each other!" Justine protested. She took a deep sigh and lamented, "This may be the last time we can be alone together."

Nothing could have prepared Michael for the word 'love.' He paced the room, his rage building with such intensity that he needed to concentrate on his breathing.

"You did not have to marry him, Justine. I am sure you knew how I felt about you," Michael said fiercely. "What the hell went through your mind?"

"What choice did I have? Would you have left your beloved church you had already devoted your life to?" she screamed.

"Yes," he yelled.

"You never said so."

"You never told me you saw a future for us—you only mentioned Smithers in your plans!"

"You should've known! Do you think I lay with every man who passes by my father's door?"

"I don't know! You tell me! Do you?" he roared at her despite full knowing that he was her first.

Justine slapped him hard across the face, and the crack echoed through the entrance hall.

"You're the same as my husband—a selfish, domineering, cruel brute."

Justine turned around and flew up the staircase like a wild, angry crackle of flame disappearing up a chimney. Michael went tearing after her taking two steps at a time. Finally, he caught up with her as she reached her bedroom.

He grabbed her roughly by the arm. She spun around and looked at him.

"What do you mean a 'brute'?" he shouted, bitterly offended by her throwaway comment. "Look at you. Do you think you would be beaten you like this if you were my wife?"

"It's none of your business."

"Never, ever, compare me with that scoundrel you chose as a husband again! Do you understand me?"

"Leave me alone, get out of this house. I never want to see you again," she cried.

"Are you sure? Is that really what you want? Or are you hiding your feelings again? You said you want a last moment with me? Do you?" he thundered arrogantly. "Because if I walk away from here today. That will never happen again."

"Get out of here, get out," she screamed back. "I have lived without you for two years, and I can carry on doing that."

But Michael adored her, and he knew that he could not leave no matter how heated the situation. She was embedded in his soul, and he would carry her with him forever. I *am sure she feels the same.*

Michael grabbed her. They were both furious with each other, but he could not stop himself from kissing her. Their fury evolved into passion. She unbuttoned his trousers, fumbling in her haste. He lifted her dress and felt the soft skin of her legs entwined around him. They were both filled with years of mutual pent-up passion, and it was all over within five wild minutes.

"This changes little. I am still livid that you didn't tell me you were questioning life in the priesthood," Justine reminded him.

"Take off all your clothes."

"I shall not!"

"Come here," he urged, with a conciliatory smile he hoped could make her heart his forever.

Reluctantly, she moved toward him. He first undressed himself and then undressed her. He was as lovely as she remembered him, and they made love repeatedly through the night. He kissed her battered face and told her how beautiful she was.

Michael insisted upon leaving late on Saturday to preach on Sunday. Too many people were relying upon him, and it was his last Sunday in the pulpit before his departure.

"Stay with me," Justine pleaded. "You can send a messenger to William, surely?"

"Is that what your husband would do? Neglect his parishioners?" he snapped.

"It's our last day together," she cried out.

"I know."

"He knew about us, you know. That's why he provoked you at the fair."

"Good."

Justine wasn't expecting the answer, and her eyes widened in disbelief.

"I love you, Michael, do you not understand that? We must be together," she beseeched.

"And is this how we will live? While your husband sits in his rectory, we hide in your father's house? I do not want to live like that."

"Leave the Catholic Church for me—for us. Please, I am begging you!"

"And then what? You'll still be married to Smithers!"

Reality had come back to bite Michael at least. He walked to the door, opened it, and left.

Justine thought to go after him then changed her mind. She slammed the door behind him. *To hell with them all. I don't need him. I don't need anybody.* She stomped off to her studio to take her frustrations out on a canvas.

William saw Michael arrive and went out to greet him.

"I take it you saw her on your rounds to the parishioners? They say he gave her a thrashing. How'd he find out then?"

"He guessed I suppose. I did spend a lot of time at the O'Leary Manor"

Michael stabled his horse then strode across the church yard. He didn't want to see anyone. He found a bottle of whiskey and went to his room, then he drank it all, hoping numbness would provide relief.

He was young, trapped in a life he didn't want with a woman he could not have. He drank until everything around him began to spin. He knew that he would feel like death behind the pulpit. *Why the feck does that matter if I leave? Or if I am pushed?* He collapsed on the floor with the empty bottle clattering down beside him. The whirling in his head did nothing to solve his problems. Mercifully for Michael, he passed out on the cold hard floor.

Later, he would thank the dear Lord that he shared a house with William. The curate found him lying on the bare flagstones in the early hours of the morning. The curate helped him to his feet, legs wobbling and weak, and together they staggered up the stairs. Michael leaned heavily on William, who took the poor inebriate to his room and dumped him onto his bed. He'd seen a lot of priests come and go, but if there was ever a 'wrong' man for the job, Michael was that man.

William had grown fond of the young fellow. He found himself wishing that he'd been brave enough to acknowledge his doubts instead of putting them away to fester. Now they'd erupted, when it was too late to do something about it.

He knew Michael was unquestionably kind-hearted and practical, but he was also firebrand. *In this institution, that would only lead to trouble. Five hundred years ago, I am sure Michael would've been burnt at the stake.*

William didn't know if things would be any easier for Michael in their point in time, but at least he would escape with his life. Then there was the matter of Justine who complicated the situation more. All that William could hope for Michael was that the Archbishop of Dublin would be understanding about the young man's dalliance with his muse.

For Michael, the hangover the following morning was grim. He stepped up to the pulpit, perspiring under his cassock. The stale taste of whiskey lurked horribly his dry mouth. His head felt like the Bunratty team football was trapped within his skull, trying to burst its way out. His temples throbbed in rhythm to his heartbeat, and he felt this last sermon was going to be the most gruelling torture he would ever endure.

In a way, it was He was saying goodbye to his first real home, to the humble people who had accepted him for what he was—and he was saying goodbye to the woman he loved.

He stood on the doorstep of the priory. William hugged him and just before they parted, gave the young man some encouraging words.

> May the wind be always at your back
> May the sun shine warm upon your face
> The rains fall soft upon your fields
> And until we meet again
> May the God who loves us all
> Hold you in the palm of his hand
> Amen.

"Thank you, William, you have always been a true friend to me. I know it has not been easy at times."

"You're going to be fine, lad. I feel in my bones the Lord has a plan for your life. With his help you will accomplish something truly great with your talents and kindness. I just know it."

Michael hoped his friend would be proved correct. For the young cleric, he felt like he was throwing his whole future into a deep, dark, lonely abyss.

He slipped away quietly, leaving the townsfolk to presume he'd been moved to another parish. If William kept quiet about his plans, he felt there was a chance everything would be just fine.

8

A PRIEST NO LONGER

Father O'Neil was filled with trepidation while he sat in a small dusty annexe outside of the archbishop's office in Dublin. The archbishop's secretary sat upright in an ornate leather chair that looked at least a thousand years old. *His assistant seems close to that age as well.* The man was formal and bristling with his body language. Michael concluded that the secretary was likely to be sour on both the best and worst of days.

The monumental building that housed the headquarters of the archdiocese was cold, and intimidating. The chilly atmosphere increased Michael's feeling of doom. Still, Michael knew that he'd reached a part of his life where he could no longer continue his priestly duties, partly due to his relationship with Justine, but mostly because he was a hypocrite preaching from the pulpit when he disagreed with so many of the church's indulgent practices.

Although Michael was a strong, intelligent man, the idea of being interviewed by someone of such seniority was daunting. He debated with himself endlessly as to what information he would disclose to the archbishop. Eventually, he decided that he would tell the truth, irrespective of the consequences. *It has to be easier in the long run than omissions and lies.*

The secretary walked to the large oak doors of the archbishop's office and turned the cast iron door handle. An eerie grinding sound echoed in the annexe. The door swung open, allowing Michael a glimpse of the room.

It was a sizeable lavish space that had luxurious red handwoven carpets on the floor, and art in broad gold frames lined the walls. The archbishop's chair was carved from mahogany and covered with all kinds of bold gilt paraphernalia that reminded him of Justine's artwork.

The secretary stood in the doorway and nodded at him, a signal that it was time to approach the room.

"Father Michael O'Neil," announced the secretary.

Then, the wizened old man leaned forward slightly towards the archbishop, in a gesture that resembled a shallow bow.

The archbishop put out his hand, and Father Michael O'Neil dutifully kissed the ring on his finger.

"Good day, your Eminence."

"Good day, Father. I understand you have travelled a long way for this interview."

Michael didn't know what he was expected to say, so he kept quiet and nodded solemnly.

The archbishop was of medium stature, with snow-white hair that was neatly groomed, but his eyes were dull and tired. Michael estimated that he was in his mid-sixties. The room confirmed the man was materialistic judging by the way he adorned his office. The young man surmised the religious community respected the archbishop because his primary concern was wealth, and he'd clearly created plenty of it.

"I am not going to waste your time Father O'Neil, but the archdiocese is most disappointed with your performance. The Bunratty parish is insolvent, and we lay the blame squarely upon your shoulders."

"I accept responsibility for the financial failure, your Eminence."

The archbishop was taken aback by the admission of guilt. He'd expected Michael to object and give him a string of excuses in an attempt to explain the problem away.

"Are you admitting that you stole and squandered the income?"

"No, your Eminence!" Michael exclaimed respectfully. "The shortfall occurred because I refused to manipulate money out of poor people who were struggling to feed themselves."

"You refused?"

"Yes, your Eminence. And I gave them practical assistance with food too."

"Your job was to teach them to rely on faith not charity, Father."

"You cannot eat 'faith', your Eminence. I know that by offering them practical help, they'd have greater faith than when I arrived," Michael said confidently.

"We taught them that they could rely on the church in times of hardship. We helped them sow their crops, fix their implements, and harvest their produce from the rain-sodden earth so that It'd not rot. And then we taught them to share their blessings."

"That sounds like a political ideology, Father, not church policy. We cannot function without tithes."

"Your Eminence, poor people cannot survive if they pay ten per cent of their meagre earnings to the richest church in the world."

"I do not like your tone, Father O'Neil. May I remind you, I can have you interred in the church cells for insubordination until you beg for forgiveness."

Michael didn't want to be arrested by the Vatican's long hand of ecclesiastical law, so he made an effort to be more diplomatic.

"I take responsibility for developing other methods of tithing. We stored grain for the winter, and the townsfolk bought fresh produce from the farmers in the summer. What those families could not give in money, they gave in kind. For the first time in fifty-two years, nobody died of starvation in my parish."

"Hmm. I suppose your method has merits, Father O'Neil. After all, Jesus did choose to feed the five thousand rather than let them go hungry. Perhaps we should invite you to share your methodology at the synod."

Michael wasn't sure if it was sarcasm or a compliment.

The archbishop turned the page of a large book in front of him, and Michael wondered how many more pages of complaints there would be about him.

"You're accused of fraternising with the nuns, Father. How do you explain that?"

Michael was losing his patience, and they were only on question two.

"There was nothing peculiar about it. We all ate meals together, which you well know is far removed from consorting together. It was an opportunity to discuss what was taking place in the parish and offer solutions to social problems. Besides, on a practical level, it was warmer in the kitchen."

The archbishop turned to the next page.

"How do you explain leaving the church for three days a week?"

"I chose to visit parishioners who had not been seen by a priest in years."

The archbishop sat up in his chair, took off his small round spectacles, and put them on the desk. He closed the big book, resigned to the fact that Michael was one of those non-conventional souls who would exhaust him with clever answers for everything.

"Of course, we can expand on all these things. In time, you will be asked to give our clerics a more detailed report of your experiences in Bunratty. The curate Father William and the Mother Superior made favourable comments about you, which are to your advantage."

"Thank you, your Eminence."

"However," cautioned the archbishop, "a more serious matter relating to your conduct has recently come to light. You have been accused of starting a brawl with Reverend Smithers from The Church of England."

"Yes, your Eminence."

"This man is the minister of the local Protestant church. You did have a fist fight in public, at a fairground. What were you thinking? You're an embarrassment to the church. Do you realise that an arbitrary loss of temper can set off sectarian unrest which we can ill afford? You'll plummet Ireland back into the acrimonious time of Cromwell."

"Yes, I agree," answered the young man.

"Father Michael, I am too old to be troubled with such things. I want to retire in peace, and my instincts are telling me that you are going to complicate the last few months of my career."

"I am sorry, your Eminence."

"I am of the mind that somebody else should be given the responsibility of disciplining you. I am already exhausted, and we have yet to read all the charges. Your acceptance of guilt is refreshing but also troublesome."

The archbishop shook his head disapprovingly.

"I understand," Michael said apologetically.

"You do?"

"Yes, your Eminence, I did run a parish, and I experienced people and their troubles every day. Something simple can quickly escalate in a major incident. I had two families who had feuded for forty—"

"—Why did you fight with the reverend, Michael?" interrupted the archbishop, his patience thinning again.

"He insulted me."

"What did he say to you?"

"He referred to me as a eunuch."

"I see. Did you punch him hard?" queried the archbishop.

"Excuse me?" said Michael, not sure if he'd heard correctly.

The old man barked his question again.

"It's quite simple, my boy. Did you hit him hard?"

"Of course," said Michael, thinking to hell with the consequences. *No lies. Just the truth.*

"Good show, Father, under those circumstances, I would've approved if you hit him twice."

Michael nodded, rather confused by the archbishop's twists and turns through what was acceptable priestly conduct and what was not.

"Please do not tell anybody what I said."

Michael wanted to laugh, but thought better of it. He was still in rather deep trouble.

> "Father O'Neil, I have met a lot of young men like you. They're dedicated to the church and to the communities that they serve, but they find it difficult to submit to the rules of the institution."

Michael nodded his head. The man had summed it up in a nutshell.

> "Tell me the truth about Paul Smithers. Let us get to the bottom of this and find a way in which you can go forward and serve the community. I doubt your only reason for hitting him was being called a eunuch. Sticks and stones and all that—"

The archbishop's voice trailed off. Michael was quiet for a very long time. He cleared his throat then began.

> "I fell in love with Justine O'Leary, who later became his wife."
>
> "Was she a Protestant?"
>
> "Yes."
>
> "That in itself is a grave sin, Michael, let alone that she is another man's spouse."

Michael began to tell the archbishop the story of Justine, much the same way that he'd told William—but without the expletives.

The archbishop sighed. The situation was not new. Red-blooded young priests often fell in love. However, most of them spent their lives, still preaching in their pulpits, haunted and guilt-ridden by their actions. They understood that without the wealth of the church behind them, life could be very unpleasant indeed.

Michael, it seemed, was not one of those men who would make do with his lot in life. He'd made up his mind that he didn't have the character to be a priest. The archbishop admired his decision, relieved that, at least, he didn't have to reform him.

> "You have broken your vows of celibacy. You have led the young Protestant woman to have a physical relationship with you before marriage, and you have committed adultery. These are grave sins in the eyes of God," the old man said soberly. "I think we can be sure that you are certainly are not a eunuch, Father O'Neil"

He continued. Michael lowered his gaze, awaiting the news of his fate.

> "With the information you have divulged, Father, I doubt that we can reform you. However, you are not a bad man at heart and you should be allowed back into regular society so that you can practice Christian goodwill on your terms."

Michael gave a sign of relief. At last, the torturous decision of his immediate future had been made.

> "I must remind you it's a long, arduous process to laicise you. With the decision to remove you from the priesthood behind us, I immediately relieve you of all your clerical duties. I will submit your case directly to Rome. Although you have some redeeming qualities, you must face the same repercussions as anybody else in this church. Unfortunately, your career as a priest has come to an end."

Relief flooded over Michael, like the great flood had covered the earth in the days of Noah. He even dared to imagine a joyful rainbow and a dove.

The archbishop interrupted his ridiculous thoughts with more details of what would happen.

> "Although you are no longer a priest, Michael, the church has educated you, and you owe us a debt of gratitude for that investment. I am going to send you to a ragged school in Manchester, where your modern, quasi-philanthropic ideas are perhaps better suited."

Michael nodded and looked at the man questioningly, hoping to learn more. He was feeling fortunate under the circumstances. It seemed he would at least have a meagre income to cover his board and lodgings somewhere.

> "Yes, with the Elementary Education Act, England is in dire need of teachers and you need to pay penance for your actions. You must complete a two-year contract of employment at

the school before you become a free man. Think of it somewhat like a short-term apprenticeship."

The archbishop put his glasses on once more and read some details from a letter on his desk.

"It's a boy's school that has been set up in Angel Meadow, one of the most impoverished slums in the city. It's called The Corning Street Technical School for Boys. There are a lot of challenges. The school needs tough young men like you. It's not a Catholic school. It's run by a committee comprised of several religious denominations. You'll be free of our influence and no longer our responsibility."

Michael listened intently, mentally mapping out what his life was going to be like.

"By far, this area is the worst slum in Northern England. It has been written about by the famous philosopher Friedrich Engels who, apparently, described as 'hell on earth'. There are thousands of Irish families living like animals. Perhaps you can redeem yourself by making it a better place for your fellow countrymen?"

9

PAYING PENANCE

The wind raged across the Irish Sea, and the temperature was low enough to form icicles that hung from the iron railings like stalactites. None of the passengers dared to expose themselves to the elements, instead, they huddled together to keep warm. The crossing in blizzard conditions was severe. Children and adults cried out from hunger, and throughout the ship, the stench of vomit, excrement and death permeated the confined spaces as people became weaker in the fierce storm.

Michael looked around him and felt pity for the poor wretches. He stared at the children and remembered his own experiences as a young boy. He'd little to comfort them with. The best he could do was give them the little food he'd with him. He was grateful that it was a relatively short journey taking a few days, unlike the poor folk transported to Australia who had to endure months of hardship onboard. Yet, the circumstances didn't improve when the passengers arrived in

Liverpool. There was no shelter from the frightful weather, and the huddled masses were no different to those who had walked from Galway to Kildare in the hope of food decades before.

Michael felt quite ashamed when he hailed a cab to transport him to the address where he would sleep, before he journeyed to Manchester.

"Master, Master! Please help me," called a woman with three small children.

"My sister lives here, and me three wee ones will freeze in the weather."

"Get in," ordered Michael.

Michael heard another desperate young couple beg him for help. He could not leave them behind to fight the harsh elements, and so he allowed them in as well. The cab driver shook his head as the carriage creaked and groaned under the strain.

"Ye bloody mad Irish man," yelled the driver.

"I will pay yer double yer normal rate," shouted Michael above the wind.

That news seemed to satisfy the man.

Michael was the first to disembark. He looked up at the large imposing building and rushed into the Anglican cathedral eager to find shelter, clutching his introduction note in his hand.

"And ye must be Michael O'Neil," called a friendly Irish voice from behind the altar.

"Yes, I am" called Michael.

"Good, let us go to the rectory and have some broth and bread. You must be famished."

A short, rotund little man with a cheeky grin and mischievous eyes appeared. He was so short that when he stood behind the altar, he could not be seen. As his voice wafted across the nave, Michael was taken by surprise.

"Father McDermott," said the cheerful little man and shook Michael's hand with a firm grip.

His jolly personality was refreshing after the stuffiness of his last days in Dublin.

"I am glad you have arrived alive."

Michael laughed.

"I am the curate. There is work in abundance here, so I am always pottering around. There is no time for shenanigans."

The little man's body jiggled as he laughed.

"Unless we are donated good grog from a loyal parishioner, then sometimes we down tools."

The humour was contagious, and as Michael's body began to thaw, so did his mood. They hunkered against the raging wind, walked through the church yard and cemetery, finally getting to a well-lit, warm rectory. A tall woman came into the warm, fire-lit parlour, then turned on her heels and left as suddenly as she arrived, her voice trailing off down the corridor.

"Father, we must feed our guest immediately. He looks rather lean after that dreadful sea crossing."

Father McDermot jiggled with laughter again.

"That is Mrs Bunting," he told Michael. "She lived hereabouts and lost her whole family during the Great Hunger. She's an angel. If you need anything, please ask her, I am not adept at housekeeping."

Ten minutes later, Mrs Bunting had laid the table. It was a simple meal of vegetable broth with fresh bread and butter. It was delicious, and the atmosphere was warm and pleasant. Michael felt content. They finished the meal with piping hot sticky-sweet tea. It was a glorious feast after the horrors of the crossing.

For the first time since Michael and Father McDermot met in the cathedral, the priest became serious.

"So, you have been given a teaching post in Angel Meadow?"

"Yes, Father, I believe you are to give me further details of the appointment. If I am honest, I only know its name and address—and that it's in a somewhat deprived area."

"Yes, unfortunately," the curate confirmed quietly.

"Why is that, Father? Can it really be any worse than the unforgivingly harsh life of rural Ireland?" Michael asked him.

"You'll be working at school with the poorest of the poor. Believe me lad, you will be entering the pits of hell."

"Which parish is that, Father?"

"That, my boy, is the surprising news. It's not attached to a parish. You'll only serve in the secular capacity of a teacher," the little man sighed. "I suppose that's probably for the best given your reason for being sent here."

Michael looked sheepish and hoped the conversation would move back to the teaching facility.

"It's the Corning Street Technical School for Boys, and you will be dealing with businessmen and politicians who support the school as well as several hundred ragged little ruffians. It'll be a considerable challenge for you."

Michael nodded.

"I know that this is a new life for you, Michael. It frees you from the Catholic church. But also, you will no longer be under its protective wing. That said, lad, the Archbishop of Dublin would never have appointed you the task if you were not up to the challenge. I doubt they want the lynching of an ex-priest on their conscience any more than a current one."

The little man gave a reassuring chuckle.

"I hope so, Father, right now, I do not know what to think or where to start."

"I hear you are quite a brawler. You'll need those boxing skills," laughed Father McDermott, circling his fists by his chest like a heavyweight champion.

Michael rolled his eyes.

"That is an overstatement, Father. It was a misunderstanding that got out of hand."

"I am sure it was," replied Father McDermott. "Now, onto more practical matters. You're welcome here anytime you need somebody to speak to, Michael. The Lord has not deserted you, rather he has put you in a position of independence and directed your skills where they'll be most valued by us earthly folk."

McDermott cleared up their tea cups.

"A tiny parish in County Clare is not where you were meant to be. You have a warrior's heart. There is a war going on deep in the slums of Manchester and you have been called up by him to fight against ignorance and poverty."

> "I do not know if I should thank you—or abscond! You sound like Henry V calling me 'unto the breach.'" confessed Michael.

Father McDermott's little body wiggled with mirth once more.

> "Come on, lad, let us get you a warm and good night's sleep. You have a great adventure ahead of you, but perhaps a final hot toddy before you settle?"

Michael agreed to the drink. Father McDermott's positivity was contagious, and by the time Michael fell asleep, he'd all the confidence he needed to face the challenge at the school in the morning.

Michael took a small commercial steamboat ride up the Mersey and Irwell Navigation and arrived at the Manchester docks at sundown. The first thing he noticed was the terrible smell permeating the harbour. The water was the colour of pea soup, and the stench that arose from it was indescribable.

He watched some desperate men fishing off the jetty. A bit further on, a child was filling a tin bucket with the ghastly liquid. He'd never seen anything as catastrophic in his life. He looked around him, and it seemed that he was the only person who noticed the putrid smell of the water. Everyone was used to it. They'd lived like this for years on end.

Michael made his way down the rickety gang-plank. The wharf was packed with men and young boys waiting for the nightshift to begin. Beggars and paupers roamed the crowd, and pickpockets identified new targets as the passengers left the ship.

Michael thought that he'd seen a lot of horror in Ireland, but felt now he was going to learn a lot more about the lower classes. He'd never lived in an industrial environment like this. He put his hands in his pockets, delighted to be free of his cassock and dog collar. It was liberating to be a new lay face about town, unrecognisable, one of many.

10

FOR BETTER OR FOR WORSE

Justine was pedantic about keeping track of her monthly cycles, and the day after Michael left, she realised that she was pregnant with her husband's child. The sliver of hope that she would ever be with Michael was destroyed. Her first thought was to abort the child. There were plenty of women in the nearby countryside who secretly operated for all classes of women.

It was an expensive and dangerous procedure, culminating in many avoidable deaths a year. On reflection, she decided she didn't want to die. Nor did she want to lie on somebody's kitchen table and suffer the public indignity of the procedure. Eventually, she discarded the idea.

As soon as Justine walked into her mother's room, Rosemary knew that her daughter was troubled. She seldom sought her mother's counsel, preferring her father's practical and less emotional approach to problems.

Justine flopped down on the chaise. She looked pale and drawn.

"Justine, are you ill? You look rather peaky."

"Mama," Justine began, "I am going to have a child. I am pregnant. I have been sick every morning for days, and I feel like I am dying."

Rosemary smiled.

"Why on earth are you looking like a thunder cloud? That is wonderful. Babies bring great joy, and your father will be delighted by the news."

Justine sighed. She didn't feel delighted. All she wanted to do was lay in her bed and disappear, taking the unwanted baby with her.

"Should we call a doctor?" asked Justine.

"Do not be over-dramatic, Justine, it's just a bit of harmless morning sickness. Keep away from rich food for the next couple of weeks, and you will begin to feel better," rosemary advised her. "I know that Mrs Shepherd up in the cottages has a thistle tea that she concocts for nausea—but first ask how many people have survived her foul brew before you drink it."

Justine laughed.

"But, let us not discuss the baby, Justine, let us discuss Michael. Is it his child?"

Justine blushed.

"No!" exclaimed Justine. "How can you ask even suggest that!"

"Fiona told me about his overnight visit, that's how."

Justine looked stunned but was grateful her mother had not gone berserk at the maid's revelation. Justine thought Fiona would've been more discreet.

"My dates are correct. It's definitely Paul's child."

"Paul's behaviour toward you has been appalling of late. The situation is a dreadful mess. After he struck you, your father refuses to accept him as a son-in-law. How are you going to live with him and give this child a happy stable home life at the same time?"

"Why are you asking Mama? I will have to go back to Paul. I have no choice."

"To my mind, the relationship with your husband has broken down irretrievably. He is not the man that you love, Justine. If you choose him, you will have to reconcile to a future that excludes a man you do have feelings for—Michael."

Justine winced again at the awkwardness of his name being brought up again.

"I didn't need Fiona to tell me. From the first moment that I saw you both together, I knew," rosemary answered.

"Are you angry?" asked Justine.

"Justine, you are a passionate woman. You have your father's determined spirit. You should never have married Paul Smithers. It would've been the same as if I had been corralled into marrying Shamus Mulroney. There would've been no passion in my life—I would've always longed for your father. I know you were trying to choose a respectable Protestant man as a husband, but Smithers is anything but respectable."

"Father will be furious."

"You don't need to worry about that," rosemary looked down to her lap to avoid eye contact then revealed, "He knows already."

"He knows? When? How?" she demanded.

"From a distance, he saw you kissing in the barn one day. He was beside himself with anger, but respected your privacy. He also likes Michael, but believed that you had no future with him being a priest and the relationship would soon fizzle out. It seems he was right once the archbishop had him removed from the parish.

Your father is more sensitive than he seems. He is terrified of you getting hurt. Will you return to Smithers? Legally, he is your husband? Although he has mistreated you for all the world to see."

"I hate him!" Justine grizzled loudly.

"It's going to be very difficult to cope on your own now you are expecting. The folks around here will expect you to be one happy family with a bairn on the way."

"I know, Mama. Despite my misgivings, I have to go back. I can't allow my hatred for Paul to taint my child's future."

"Do you need your father's help?"

"I don't think that Paul will beat me again now Michael is gone. I have to tell him about the baby," she answered. "Perhaps it'll warm his heart to me again."

"But it'll not warm your heart Justine, and you know that."

Justine's carriage stopped outside the rectory, where she'd been living a dejected and miserable life. She climbed a few worn granite steps and rapped her gloved knuckles on the front door. Paul heard the knock. It was the maid's afternoon off, so he'd to answer the door himself. He manoeuvred himself out of his chair with great difficulty, each movement of his leg sending red hot pain through his body. He reached for his crutches and slowly made his way to the door.

When Paul finally opened the entrance, he was pale, and perspiration ran down his face. He looked at Justine. He noticed her face had healed except for a small scar on her cheek.

He didn't greet her or invite her into the house. Instead, he left the door open and hobbled back to his seat, one agonising step at a time. He collapsed into his chair next to the fire and took some deep breaths. Answering the door had exhausted him.

Justine went into the house and closed the door behind her. She walked into the familiar parlour, without waiting to be invited, and sat down on the small settee, a beautiful piece of furniture that she'd chosen when they got married.

> "So, you are returning, like the dog you are, with your tail between your legs?" Paul said with bitterness and hatred. "Oh, how the mighty have fallen."

Justine looked at him, wishing that she'd crushed his skull instead of his kneecap.

> "Michael O'Neil has left, and you are ready to become a wife again, are you?" he sneered.

Justine kept quiet. She'd inflicted her revenge. A war of words would be meaningless.

"What do you want? You have crippled me for the rest of my life. Do you think I will ever take you back? I will see you starve on the street and walk past you without mercy."

Justine looked straight into his eyes without flinching.

"I am having our marriage annulled on the grounds of you not performing your wifely duties, your physical responsibilities that is. I have set the procedure in motion, and the annulment will be published within a month. I have the full support of the courts and the church."

Justine didn't take her contemptuous gaze off him. Paul looked at her with venom in his eyes. If he were strong enough, he would've beat her to within an inch of her life and dumped her on her father's doorstep, broken and damaged. He would beat her so savagely to ensure that she would never have children.

She looked at him and felt no pity. He'd crossed the boundary of decency when he'd beaten her. In a strange way she was grateful. Had it not been for that cruelty, she would still be with him and loyal to her marriage vows. She was prepared to sacrifice the man she loved, a man no longer in the priesthood, for a husband she deplored.

Justine could leave him to his harsh bitterness, but she'd to think of the child. He'd no idea of the favour that he would bestow upon her by pursuing an annulment. Yet, she was in no position to take advantage of his proposal.

If he shunned his child, he would've to resign from the clergy, he would never let that happen. In public at least, he would play the part of a good husband if only to retain his social status.

"What do you have to say for yourself, you shrew?" he spat.

"I am pregnant," she said without wasting words.

Paul put his head back and gave a cynical laugh.

"You mean you are pregnant with Michael O'Neil's child."

"No, it's your child."

Paul Smithers stared at her, trying to reconcile his thoughts. It suddenly dawned on him that if Justine had his child, she would never leave him, and she could never be with Michael O'Neil. There would be many ways to make her pay for what she'd done to him. He was determined to make sure her life was a misery. Michael O'Neil would never leave his new life for a married woman with a child fathered by a man he despised. Losing her lover would torture her forever, and Paul would ensure that he would rub salt in that wound every day of her life.

"You may come back," he said with resentment in his voice, "but do not expect a warm welcome. I am doing you a great favour. I am saving your reputation. From now on you will be at my disposal till the day I decide to discard you, like the dirt that you are."

"Thank you," Justine snarled.

"You can start by kissing me goodbye."

It was the worst demand that he could have asked of her. She walked toward him, revolted, and stooped to kiss him on his cheek. She could feel his rough stubble against her lips. He grabbed her by the hair and pulled her mouth down toward him, covering her mouth with his. Justine felt her stomach heave. He thrust his arm, and she toppled over in shock.

"That is just a foretaste of my expectations. I do not have to beat you to destroy you."

As Justine got off her knees, for the first time in her life, she felt thoroughly defeated. Nevertheless, she'd her child to consider. If Paul took the risk of having their marriage annulled, the baby would be treated as a bastard, and its future would be doomed. Michael had left her behind. She could not count upon him to rescue her. He was bound to be wedded to his new life.

Paul was filled with hatred for Justine. The most profound sorrow consumed Justine as she realised, she would never again have the love and passion that she'd experienced with Michael.

*

"Good God, Justine," muttered Douglas O'Leary, clenching his jaw to prevent himself from shouting at her.

"Father, I must return to Paul."

"He is vermin."

"This bairn must know its father. Surely you understand that, Papa?"

"What about Michael? He was besotted with you. He will surely accept you. And he will accept the child. Let Paul Smithers get an annulment."

"I can never demand or expect that from Michael. He deserves his own family."

"You adore the man, Justine, and he is in love with you."

"But he has stopped contacting me! Doesn't that tell you enough? I presume he has forgotten all about me as he settles into his new parish."

"He is more honourable than you believe, Justine. You led him around the gooseberry bush, and it was your fault that he struggled to commit himself to you. We all knew he railed against a lot of the demands placed on him by the archbishop and the Vatican."

"It was my fault that I married Paul Smithers. He was the wrong choice. How could I commit to a man who loved himself more than me? I was little more than a trophy."

"Justine, we will raise the child under this roof. I am not ashamed to do so. Anything is preferable to you being that man's punchbag!" bellowed Douglas.

"I do not care if I hate my husband, but I cannot deny my child a father. It'll carry a stigma for the rest of its life, ridiculed, insulted."

"Start thinking, Justine, you are not only responsible for yourself anymore. That baby will never experience a happy family under that man's roof. Plenty of men take on another fellow's child as his own. My priority is that you and the child are loved—and that will never happen with that selfish cad, Smithers."

Justine looked at her father, a single tear ran down her cheek. She knew that her father loved her, and he was right. Douglas O'Leary was a remarkable man, father, and husband, and it was seldom that he chastised her.

"I can't, Father. I can't ignore the facts."

"Go then! Be stubborn. Go back to the mean little swine if you won't accept my help. But let me remind you he will make your life a living nightmare. You may feel you can withstand the abuse, but there is no guarantee that I will tolerate him using his fists on you again. Especially when you are expecting my grandchild. You're putting me in a position where I will murder him if he ever hurts you again. You have only crippled one leg. He still has the rest of his body, of which. I will joyously break bone for bone."

"It was my fault, Papa. I was not a virgin when I married. He'd every right to feel betrayed by me—and Michael when he'd put two and two together."

Douglas was uncomfortable hearing this deeply private information and struggled to look at her. He simmered in silence for a while, but eventually weakened and put his consoling arms around his daughter.

"I know you are your own woman, but if you or the baby are in any danger, I will fetch you. This is your home and you are safe here. Promise me you will always remember that."

She nodded, tears running down her face.

*

Justine entered the confessional. When Father William slid the screen open, he was surprised to see her.

"I suppose you are here to repent," he asked with a wry smile.

"No, Father. It's something more important than that. I need to know where Michael is," replied Justine.

William had anticipated the visit. Michael had not asked the curate to keep his whereabouts a secret it from Justine. He secretly believed that would both find security in knowing each other's whereabouts. It seemed to him that they would always gravitate toward one another, whatever the distance or challenge.

"He has written to me, Justine. He is in Manchester, working in a slum called Angel Meadow."

"I will never see him again," she whispered.

"How can you say that?"

"Because he chose the priesthood over me, and now he lives in England, even a platonic rendezvous is out of the question."

"That is where you are wrong, my dear. Do you know that he is no longer a priest?"

Justine's mouth fell open in joyous disbelief.

"He confessed your relationship to the archbishop— which took a great amount of courage, I might add. He has been laicised."

"What does that mean?" she asked.

"He is no longer a priest, but on the archbishop's instruction, he has been appointed to a school for boys in the most hellish place on earth as penance, for—well, I think you know what that might be."

"He did not write to me. How do I know you are telling the truth?"

"He gave up. He believed that he could never have you and thought it best to move on."

Justine had stopped listening, trapped in her own world of horror.

"I am pregnant with my husband's child," she blurted out. "And that means Michael, and I will never be together again. He won't want me now. I will mourn him every day for the rest of my life."

"It's a very complicated situation. As a religious man, I must instruct you to honour your marriage vows. Until do you part. The child will comfort you, Justine. Focus on the baby for now, and make the child your priority."

Justine left the church feeling betrayed. She climbed into the carriage. She was engulfed by sadness, and she began to weep softly. Moments later, she began to sob like a child. Her heart was broken. Eventually, the driver stopped the carriage and opened the door.

"Miss Justine, do you need my help? You seem so very troubled."

Ryan O'Connor had worked for her father for many years. The old man had known her since she was born. He knew that Justine was a strong woman. Whatever was tearing her heart to shreds must mean the world to her. He climbed into the carriage and have her white gloved hand a reassuring squeeze and dabbed at her tears with his handkerchief.

"Come lass, come now. I am taking you home to your father."

Justine allowed herself to be consoled. She'd no energy to be proud. She was broken.

Douglas O'Leary accompanied Justine back to the rectory. He would not allow her to return alone because he did know what his rat of a son-in-law was capable of doing.

Paul Smithers put out his hand to greet Douglas. He was dressed in his frock, ready to preach a mid-morning service. Douglas O'Leary ignored his feigned polite gesture.

"Do you see the physical condition in which I deliver my daughter today?" **Douglas** asked in a booming voice that the whole household could hear.

Reverend Paul Smithers nodded.

"If she ever arrives at my home battered, I will break all the bones in your body, and then I will hang you on a meat hook for the whole town to see."

Paul Smithers remained quiet. O'Leary was not a man to be challenged. He grabbed the frock coat collar and pulled the reverend towards him roughly.

"I will kill you, even if it means the gallows for me. Do you understand what I am saying?" **Douglas** snarled in his ear.

Paul nodded as the old man released his grip.

"You'll not withhold any of the former privileges she'd under my roof, and you will create space in this massive gloomy hole for her to pursue her career as an artist."

"She's my wife, and this is my house," Paul answered firmly in an attempt to maintain his authority.

O'Leary grabbed him by his dog collar.

"I am her father, and I did not give her to a husband to be destroyed. She has chosen to come back to you—God alone knows why. If it were up to me, she would never see you again."

"She'd already lost her virginity to Michael 'O'Neil when we were engaged. Then, she broke her marriage vows and became an adulteress with him after our wedding."

"Good for her, you runt. At least she has experienced the love of a real man. Michael O'Neil is a greater man than you can ever be. I am sorry that she could not marry him."

The staff were staggered by what they were hearing. It was scandalous. The servants had never known anyone to hold such immoral opinions. It was almost too shameful to repeat. Nobody would believe that such a conversation had ever taken place.

Still, it gave them a thrill to listen to the violence, slander, and unashamed support of Douglas O'Leary for the immoral behaviour of his daughter, the wife of Reverend Paul Smithers.

Douglas O'Leary kissed his daughter on the forehead. He wanted to cry as he watched her walk up the stairs to the marital bedroom, fearless and brave, her wild dark hair floating behind her. His heart broke for her. He knew what he'd felt for Rosemary, and he knew that Justine had the same strength of feeling for Michael. He was sure that she was suffering right down to the core of her being.

*

Michael stood at the entrance of his temporary lodgings and looked up at the façade, which was neat and painted, in stark contrast to the other ramshackle and rundown buildings in the area. It was icy cold, but that was all his senses could register about the wider environment.

Without his watch, he could not tell if it was day or night. Here and there, warm yellow lamplight shone through the dusty windows on the housing rows. Except for those patches of light, thanks to the heavy smog, a hazy twilight permanently hung over the maze of streets, creating a sense of gloom.

The only place the temperature rose a little was outside the factories that had coal-driven machinery. Groups of bony half-starved people huddled together to benefit from the warmth that leaked out from the factory doors and vents, while others lit open fires in sheltered corners to keep warm.

Michael trudged up the hill. It wasn't raining, but a sludgy brown liquid was flowing down the street, making its way downhill to the River Irk. He was disgusted when he saw a woman empty her chamber pot onto the road. The foul contents splashed onto his boots. It was only then that he realised the stinking liquid running down the street was raw sewage. Michael was appalled. He'd watched people starve and struggle in Ireland. He'd witnessed rural poverty and exploitation, but these folks were beyond impoverished. The slums were a living cesspool of urban decline, disease, and death. He identified various accents as he walked along and noted most of them were Irish.

Michael reached a red-brick civic building with a small badge at the door which read:.

The Corning Street Technical School for Boys.

Although the school interior was neatly painted, and the woodwork cared for, the exterior was dirty with soot, the red brick almost black. It was impossible to see through the grubby windows. Next to the school, Michael had been horrified to see an empty plot used as a dumping ground for animal and human waste that was being sold as compost.

He stood on the steps in front of the green doors. It took all his self-discipline not to turn and run, perhaps to take a punt on finding some day work in an engineering workshop.

The squalor made him want to go back to Ireland and beg Douglas O'Leary for a job. However, he reasoned that he'd been given a challenge. He still owed a debt to the church that saved his life, educated, and protected him. Besides, if the archbishop caught wind of him absconding on his first day, he would be in even more trouble.

With a resigned nod, Michael opened the door and took his first steps into another world.

11

THE CORNING STREET TECHNICAL SCHOOL FOR BOYS

Michael O'Neil introduced himself and shook the headmaster's hand. Mr Burbidge was somewhat surprised at the man's stature. He'd not expected a tall, well-built Irishman who looked like a Celtic warrior.

"Welcome to our school Father O'Neil," a grateful Mr Burbidge replied.

"Call me Michael."

"Excuse me?" said Mr Burbidge.

"I do not enjoy the ceremony, sir, please call me Michael. And these days, I am Mr O'Neil."

"Well, this is all rather strange. I thought we were getting Father Michael O'Neil," said the headmaster, a question in his voice.

"I was a priest, sir, now I am a teacher. I am hardworking and keen to make a start. You can rely on me."

"As you know," said Mr Burbidge, "this is a school for boys. I asked for a teacher who was competent in engineering—not just theology and Latin. These boys need to be taught factory skills."

Michael laughed easily.

"In rural Ireland, having some skills was a bonus. They church was keen for me to offer practical help, not just parade to and from the pulpit. Between you and I, I preferred engineering, which is probably why the archbishop sent me here."

As he said 'engineering,' he remembered Justine, and he became aware of his lie.

"What age are the boys that I will teach, Mr Burbidge?"

"The boys are of all ages. They're orphans that have been taken off the streets."

Michael nodded, pleased that even in the squalor of the slum, someone saw fit to nurture the needy.

"We'll only give you the brightest and most well-behaved boys—the ones that can already read, write and count. We do not want to waste your talents on young men who have no intellect."

"I do not want to teach only the brightest children, Mr Burbidge. You do not need to read and write to know where to tap things with a hammer."

"Even though we call this a technical school, Father, excuse me, Michael," **Burbidge** corrected himself, "it's just a nicer name for a normal ragged school. We have many aristocrats, politicians, and clergy that support this little community, and we have boys as young as five years old living in the hostel."

"Hostel?" Michael said. "I did not know that you had a hostel attached to this school."

"Yes, the most gifted boys are housed in the attic. They're looked after to the best of our ability. As I said, there are a lot of very prominent men who keep our institution running. The building may look terrible outside but it's comfortable inside. We provide moral guidance, good food, warmth, and education."

"It's inspiring to know that there are people who care," Michael added.

"Oh, yes, you will often see them here. Some of them even pop in and see the little chaps in the evenings."

"Would you mind showing me where I will be teaching and living. I was told that the post included accommodation."

"Indeed, it does," said Mr Burbidge. "Let me first show you your classroom.

Michael was led down a long cold whitewashed corridor with creaky wooden floors. His classroom was a large room with enough benches to seat thirty boys. A chalkboard stood at the front of the room. A wobbly pile of slates was stacked on top of each other on the floor. The classroom was freezing. There was a fireplace, but no fire. Other than the basics, the room was very bare indeed. Michael felt underwhelmed by his new working conditions.

"Just getting the children to take classes is a challenge," Mr Burbidge told Michael. "Some of them will live here for a short while and then run away or disappear. I cannot understand why they leave. It's a big problem. That is why I suggested that you focus on the most compliant scholars."

Michael bristled at the use of the word 'compliant.' For some reason, he could not put his finger on he associated it with the sort of suffocating control he'd experienced in the Catholic Church. He shrugged it off and put his feelings down to his rebellious nature, but Michael was an astute man with good instincts. Listening to people's confessions for so many years had taught him a lot, and he was sensitive to manipulation.

His living quarters were small and sparse. It was comprised of a 'main' room barely big enough to store his bed, and a small study area in a tiny annexe with a window so high up, that he would've to burn an oil lamp throughout the day to see what he was doing. There was a water closet down the hallway, which he'd to share with a few other staff members who also lived there. There were also some even small cellars in the basement used for storage.

Michael felt as if he were in jail. He'd not felt this sorry for himself since he watched his parents die on the side of the road. Ireland had considerable shortcomings, but he missed the green hills and fresh air of his old parish. He even missed the rain. At that moment, Michael would've given anything to return 'home'. He'd promised himself that he would curtail his thoughts of Justine, but try as he might, he could not. True, he missed her, but he knew that he was a clinging fantasy, not a future.

He caught himself before he became entirely swamped by his melancholy and was thankful for the distraction of the dinner bell that clanged loudly somewhere in the building.

He made his way down the rickety staircase, terrified that he would fall through the worn planks. Relieved to survived the trip down two flights of stairs, as he reached the bottom, a fat man with layers of jowls dripping down his face introduced himself as the 'hostel master'—Mr Hayes.

He shook Michael's hand and welcomed him in a friendly manner, then pointed him towards a dining room filled with boys.

As the headmaster had said, Michael estimated them to be as young as five years and as old as sixteen. There approximately fifty children, far more than he'd expected.

"I was expecting a priest," said Mr Hayes.

Michael brushed the comment off with a chortle. He didn't feel like explaining himself again.

The headmaster's table seated five men: the headmaster, the hostel master, two teachers, and Michael. Except for the headmaster, these were all people who lived on the premises. The two teachers were young men in their mid-twenties, and they didn't look very experienced. In fact, they seemed quite intimidated by their elders. Michael supposed they'd been gifted students who had stayed on to learn how to instruct. The young teachers introduced themselves as Grant Conrad and Harry Joyce.

The boys lined up for their dinner, then walked to their tables. The quantity and quality of the food was surprisingly good for a charitable organisation. The dining hall was deadly quiet. Each child ate his dinner in silence. The only noise was the sound of cutlery scraping and clinking against the plates they ate off.

"How many lads are there?" Michael asked Harry.

"Just over fifty. Some are very young. Since it's now law that the little ones get a few hours of education a day, we have developed them well. But the older ones. Well, they have been working since the age of eight or nine. They have become independent and have fended for themselves, so we struggle to keep them on the straight and narrow. They think they're men who know everything about the grown-up world of work," harry answered.

Michael nodded and took a sip of his tea.

"How long have you taught here, Harry?"

"Conrad, and I joined at the same time, approximately two months ago now. There are other staff as well, and they live in the rooms on the same floor as us. The boys are one floor above us in the attic. You'll notice that they're well-disciplined and restrained at night, not running amok thankfully."

"Hayes is in charge of the boys' day-to day-living needs. He has a few older chaps that help him. They're a bit too rough around the edges for my liking. They also live up there," said Joyce.

"Yes," said Conrad, "we were recruited from the Midlands. Nobody told us we were coming to hell itself. It was pitched as a glorious opportunity. It's alright in here I suppose, but out there on the streets it's bedlam."

"Yes, I noticed as I walked over this morning."

"We heard that you were a priest," asked a smiling Harry.

"I was a priest, but that didn't really go to plan. Perhaps, I will be a better teacher," Michael added with a cheeky wink. "At least I hope so, I am to be here for two years!"

It was then Michael focused his entire being on becoming the perfect teacher.

12

THE BLESSING OF ROSIE JOY

The scandalous news of Reverend Smither's wife shook the small Bunratty community like an earthquake. They never had and would never experience such salacious gossip like that which they heard from the rectory staff ever again.

The news even reached the small convent and the nuns—bless their holy souls—were as intrigued by the behaviour of Father Michael O'Neil as any of the other folk in the area. Smithers milked the situation for all the sympathy he could raise, and his congregation would've given him a sainthood for taking back his errant wife if they'd enough influence over the canonisation process.

While the reverend continued to preach about adultery at the Protestant church, Father William was getting bored of hearing constant confessions. Women were having sinful thoughts and conversations about the matter. They even confessed the sin of their increased desires to experience the physical acts perpetrated by the adulterers. Father William was convinced that he was privy to a suppressed moral revolution. If Paul Smithers were aware of how much silent support was being meted toward the adulterers, he would've left Bunratty and taken a ship to Australia.

The bitter cleric repeatedly lectured on the subject of adultery and forgiveness for six consecutive Sundays. Eventually, the church council members suggested that the congregation needed guidance in other facets of spirituality as well, and that perhaps it was time to change the subject. They felt the parishioners had got the message, and he'd made his point. Smithers felt somewhat affronted but obeyed the instruction resentfully. He felt it was another instance of him being the wounded party in a relationship.

Justine Smithers sat in the front row of the church, her pregnancy showing more and more each week.

Gossip abounded on whether it was Michael or Paul's child, and Father William instructed his congregation to put an end to the pointless tittle-tattle.

In public, Smithers doted upon his pregnant, erring and yet forgiven wife. The pedestal the congregation placed him on had grown significantly higher over the last tumultuous weeks. He was admired by them all for his ability to put the terrible disgrace and betrayal behind him, to be calm, stoic, unflappable, and put the spiritual needs of others ahead of his own.

People attended the services as if they were there to read the next chapter of an exciting book. Some Catholics began attending the Protestant church just to keep up with the latest news, and Father William had to threaten them with the fury of the Pope and the bowels of hell to get them to stop.

Still, the curate's most significant irritation was the number of confessions he'd to deal with after they'd visited the 'enemy'.

Although Justine displayed public humility over this period, she carefully noted which people relished in her misery. At heart, Justine was a kind soul, but she could not suffer hypocrisy. She'd been publicly renounced and tarnished by the so-called Christians in the village. If it were not that her husband had taken her back, and that her father was 'hellfire' incarnate, she would likely have been tarred and feathered.

She spent almost all day in the attic at the rectory, pursuing her art. But what she was producing had become dark and disturbing, a distinct reflection of her frustrated desire to fight back at her oppressors.

Worse than the gloomy creative works, she felt it difficult to feel any enthusiasm for the child that she was going to mother. Rosemary repeatedly reminded her of the 'blessing' she'd received. Her father was beside himself with excitement at being a grandfather again, even if he loathed Smithers. Still, Justine could not conjure up any positive emotions. She bore resentment toward her husband, who wore his potency like a badge. She felt that he'd beaten her twice. First, physically, and secondly, by impregnating her with his child, which would keep Justine linked to him forever, whether she liked it or not.

She lay next to the odious Smithers every night since she'd moved back to the rectory. He'd insisted that Justine perform her marital duties while she was pregnant. He'd never been overtly physical before, but now he saw it as a conquest, and she was required to capitulate once or even twice a night.

Her cruel husband's desire was not fuelled by lust, but rather to wield power and to crush her spirit for good. He knew that she hated him, and he ensured that it hurt her every time.

Even when she was several months into her pregnancy, he delighted in forcing her into more undignified positions to satisfy himself and to humiliate her.

The baby was born on a Sunday. Justine went into labour early in the morning, and the reverend left her to preach to his congregation. He didn't care to attend the birth. It meant nothing except another way to control his wife.

While he stood behind the pulpit, he prayed that Justine would suffer the most excruciating labour and to die in childbirth. In his twisted mind, death was the perfect punishment for her sins against him.

He announced to the church, to a multitude of accompanying gasps and whispers, that his wife was in the throes of giving birth to their child.

This was to be the start of another chapter in the life of the minister and his wife.

Reverend Paul Smithers was invited to luncheon, tea and then dinner, all on the precept of keeping him calm and cared for by the ladies in the congregation, while his wife gave birth with the doctor and midwife.

The birth of the child was over within twelve hours, born at the precise moment that Paul was hoping that Justine would die. The staff had summoned her mother and father, and they arrived to find Justine holding the tiniest bundle in her arms.

Justine's eyes were bright, her hair fanned across the pillows, and she was delighted that her husband was absent. The entire birth had been her sole experience, and he was unable to take any credit for supporting her. Her long-standing indifferent feelings to the bairn had gone. The child was totally and absolutely Justine's precious gift to herself. From the moment Justine set eyes on the baby, screaming, pink, eyes firmly closed with a shock of black hair, she wondered why she'd ever thought that she would not love her own flesh and blood.

As the young girl suckled on her mother, Justine's wonder grew and to add to her fulfilment. She realised that she carried the nourishment and the strength that the little girl would need for the rest of her life, not just until she was weaned.

"What will you name her?" asked Douglas O'Leary.

"Joy," Justine smiled. "Rosemary Joy—"

She stopped speaking, struggling to say the surname. Her heart tore apart at the thought of Michael.

"Smithers," added Justine, with a lump in her throat.

Douglas O'Leary was the first person to pick her up. Justine beamed. Rosie was in good hands.

13

THE NO NONSENSE MAN

Michael stood in front of a class of thirty hooligans that paid no attention to him at all. Mr Burbidge took advantage of Michael's comment that all boys could be educated with technical skills with the right encouragement. He was relieved to get rid of them and put them in Michael's classroom. Mr Burbidge ensured that the class was full of horrors.

Michael took some time watching the interactions between the lads, gauging who were friends, bullies and bullied. The older chaps definitely terrorised the little ones, but there were a few cunning and streetwise urchins who knew how to play the game and avoid victimisation.

Eventually, Michael put his fingers in his mouth and whistled, like a shepherd would call his border collie. For the lads, it was the type of sound that they would've heard on the street, but louder and more piercing, making some of the boys put their hands over their ears.

They realised that this teacher was not like any of the others they'd ensured to date. Most of the priests who had taught them were soft and easy to intimidate. The sheer size and gruffness of the man made them think twice about disobeying.

The shrill whistle had the desired effect, and they all turned around and looked at the tall, commanding man standing at the front of the classroom.

"Hey you, geezer, ye ain't a priest? Where is the priest we were s'posed to get?" yelled a child of approximately six years.

He looked into the boy's eyes. The cheeky little hooligan had a big mouth. It was evident that his poor environment and the lack of a father, accompanied by the necessity to fend for himself on the streets, had matured him way beyond his years. Michael was not going to coax the class into obedience. He decided that would not work. Firm decisive action was required. Instead, he looked straight into the eyes of the young man.

"Sit down!" Michael thundered.

All the boys sat down at once.

"I am Mr O'Neil, and I am your new teacher. What is the first rule of the day?" Michael said fiercely.

"We have to pray?" suggested somebody in the middle of the classroom.

"No," Michael bellowed.

He'd all the boys' attention now. It was extraordinary to get a priest who didn't insist on prayer.

"The first rule is to get a fire going and warm us all up."

The pupils looked at each other uneasily. One of the older boys at the back of the class piped up.

"We ain't allowed to make a fire, Sir. The school can't afford the sweeps."

"And the coal costs too much, sir," added another.

"From today on, we make a fire, and we will sweep our own chimney."

Michael took a coal scuttle and went to Mr Burbidge's office.

"I have thirty cold and hungry boys in my classroom Mr Burbidge, and I am going to fetch coal out of the cellar for a fire."

Mr Burbidge cleared his throat in preparation for a polite confrontation.

"Mr O'Neil, we do not light fires in our classrooms, some children are only here for two hours a day, and then they go out to their jobs at the factories."

Michael put the coal scuttle on the headmaster's desk and walked over to the warm fire burning in the man's office. He rubbed his hands in front of it, all the while watching the scuttle, without saying a word. The message was subtle, but the headmaster caught on.

"Go ahead then, Mr O'Neil, go and get your coal if that is what you want to do."

"Thank you, sir," replied Michael with a smile.

For the boys in the classroom, this act was the first indication that they were not working with just any man. This was a 'no nonsense' man. The fire warmed them up, and they realised that Mr O'Neil cared about their comfort a lot more than the others in charge of the school.

"What is your name?" Michael called out to a lad of about sixteen.

"Peter," the boy yelled back at him.

"Come here!" Michael ordered.

Peter walked to the front of the class. He'd a smarmy over-confident attitude. Michael watched the younger boy's faces and noted the hint of fear in their eyes.

"From now on you refer to me as 'Sir.' Do we understand each other," warned Michael in a normal tone.

"Whatever you say, Mister, but do not yer bovver me and me boys too much. We only listen to Mr Hayes."

"Who are the other boys here who only listen to the hostel master?" asked Michael.

Three of Peter's friends stood up. They were all dressed in similar clothing. Their trousers and jackets were not the same. Still, the four young men wore the same flat caps, scarves, and clogs. Michael knew nothing about the scuttler gangs that ran the Manchester streets, and it was to his advantage.

Peter and his friends stood in front of Michael, who towered over them.

"You give us any bovver, mate, and we will take care of you."

"Where do you four live?" Michael asked.

"S'got nothin' te do wiv ya." said one lad, grinning to the class.

"We lives upstairs, we do," answered Peter.

"Are you here to learn?"

"Nope! We here te keep law and order."

Michael smiled at them, and the four young men that thought that they'd him beat.

"Well, then you are unnecessary," said Michael.

"Wadda ya mean, guv? Why yer saying that then?"

"Because I only have people in my classroom who want to learn. And from now on, I keep law and order—not you."

The four little thugs looked at him aghast. Peter shook his head.

"Yer dunna want te know what you just got yersel' into, Mister, but it ain't going to be nice fer yer when old Hayes calls yer in."

Michael ignored Peter and opened the door for them to leave.

"Ye dunna understand, Priest. Hayes is gonna have ya blood."

Michael watched the other scholars out of the corner of his eye. The mention of Hayes had made them feel uncomfortable. They'd dropped their eyes to their desks and started to fidget nervously.

Peter was the last scuttler of the four to pass the new teacher. Even though he knew that he was no match for Michael, Peter still took a chance at giving him a shove. A strong man from spending all those years in Ireland working with the farmers, he picked Peter up and threw him out of the classroom.

The remaining boys wanted to cheer in their **seats**, but they did not dare. They were too terrified.

14

THE FIGHT FOR FAIRNESS

"Mr O'Neil, this is Lord Sedgefield and Bishop Donkin of the Church of England," said Burbidge.

He shook their hands warmly. He'd expected that he would be formally introduced to the board of trustees eventually.

"Michael, these gentlemen are two out of a governing body of seven. They take responsibility for financing our successful institution," the headmaster said in a patronising tone.

"Unfortunately, the others cannot be here tonight. Mr Hayes, and I serve on the same body. It's imperative to have people who are in management positions at the school all day. We ensure that everything works efficiently," said Mr Burbidge nervously.

"I understand," replied Michael.

"As you know, this governing body has created a haven where orphans and the helpless can live in comfort. Have you seen the boys' quarters in the attic yet?"

"No, sir, I have not been on a formal tour."

"You're free to visit their quarters whenever you wish," instructed Burbidge.

"Thank you, sir, I will arrange for someone to accompany me on my visit. I will ask Mr Conrad and Mr Joyce."

Lord Sedgefield and Bishop Donkin stood on each side of the fireplace like sentinels guarding a fortress, and they'd not said a word since Michael arrived.

"Let us have a drink in celebration of your appointment," spluttered the headmaster in an attempt to ease the tension in the room.

All three men moved toward Mr Burbidge's desk and sat down.

"Father O'Neil, we are delighted to have you as a spiritual light in the dark life of these little urchins," said Bishop Donkin.

"I am no longer a priest, Bishop. I was appointed to this post by the Archbishop of Dublin, but not as a priest, but rather a secular teacher, specialising in engineering."

The bishop frowned and glanced at Lord Sedgefield.

"This is indeed a complication," griped Lord Sedgefield. "We were very particular about the qualifications required for the appointment."

"Why is there so much value attached to appointing a priest?" asked Michael.

"Well, we believe that the boarders at the school must feel free to speak to somebody in confidence if they're unhappy with anything here. Whatever their denomination, the clergy seem to put them at ease."

Michael nodded in agreement. Lord Sedgefield continued.

"We prefer it to be somebody who can analyse their complaints from the right perspective."

"And what perspective is that, S—?"

"—From the perspective of the school," interrupted Archbishop Donkin.

"I met the youngsters in my class today, and they didn't have any difficulty in communicating. The little hooligans were quite outspoken, in fact," Michael added.

"Yes, yes, and that is why we need somebody who is discreet. They're children way beyond their years, and we need somebody who can treat their complaints with discretion," said Lord Sedgefield.

"I do not have to be a priest to respect people's privacy," said Michael with a hint of irritation. "I believe that the same would apply to Mr Conrad and Mr Joyce. We are professional people who are appointed as educators because we have advanced qualifications. We have academic pedigrees, sir, and we do not need to be questioned on our ethics."

Lord Sedgefield grew red in the face, and it was evident that he didn't appreciate Michael's honesty, nor was he used to being contradicted. Burbidge, the headmaster, sensed the tension between the two men, and he subtly headed the conversation toward a different, but far more controversial topic.

"I am much more concerned about what happened in your classroom this morning," Mr Burbidge said in a confident voice. "I had a complaint from Mr Hayes, and he is livid."

"What happened?" asked Bishop Donkin.

"Michael saw fit to expel four young men from his class. It's Peter and the other three who we have employed to protect the young boys and guarantee their safety. "

"That is completely unacceptable," boomed Lord Sedgefield.

As all eyes suddenly turned to him, he realised his overreaction and dropped his voice to its average pitch.

"Peter, Frank, Andrew and Fred have been with the school for years. They escort the young children to and from work to ensure their safety. Some of the nine-year-olds who work in the cotton mills are subject to danger on these terrible streets. We are off to an awful start if you believe you may expel people as you wish," complained the archbishop. "Especially when they have a track record for protecting the boys."

"Gentlemen, with all due respect," countered Michael calmly, "I will not have sixteen-year-old thugs sitting in my classroom intimidating the younger lads, and worse trying to intimidate me. I am employed to do the best that I can to nurture this community so that these young men have a better future with better skills. "

"Who do you think you are—?" the bishop began.

Michael did not allow him to finish. He was so sick of the clergy that he could no longer show much respect toward them.

"Bishop, I do not tolerate bullies, and I will thrash the living daylights out of anybody who dares stand in my way of giving the lessons, which you have employed me to do."

They could not believe their ears. Their heads spun around to look at him. The headmaster began to fumble around with things on his desk. Everybody put their unfinished drinks down.

"I will not waive the safety of this institution because of one of your whims, Michael" said Lord Sedgefield in an uppity voice.

"The young men will be reinstated as prefects, but they'll not attend classes."

"They're the same nuisances for Mr Conrad and Mr Joyce."

"Very well then, that is decided, the scholars do not need protection in the classroom, but they'll be escorted on the streets and overseen in their dormitories. Mr Hayes cannot function without their help."

"Thank you," said Michael.

The bishop and Lord Sedgefield left the room without saying goodbye Michael. And Michael left the room without a farewell to Mr Burbidge.

Mr Burbidge put his head in his hands. Michael O'Neil was trouble.

"We may have employed the wrong man," Donkin said to Sedgefield out in the corridor.

"I can understand why the Catholics wanted to get rid of him," said Sedgefield. "He is like a wild animal. Thoroughly uncontrollable."

"Yes," Donkin said, "he was not what I had in mind. I thought that they would appoint somebody more compliant, more flexible."

"If he becomes a problem, we will return him to Dublin," said Sedgefield.

"You do not understand, Sedgefield. It appears Michael O'Neil is affiliated to the church, and he will remain a brother for the rest of his life, but he does not report to them. Due to his laicisation, he is a free man."

"How the hell did we not know this when we appointed him?"

"I don't know what Burbidge was doing, but we cannot get rid of him yet, it's too soon. Burbidge will smell a rat."

15

DESTINED TO FOLLOW

From the moment that Smithers saw his daughter, he hated her. As the days passed, and she grew little by little, Rosie became a replica of her mother. Her bright little eyes twinkled, and her dark hair made her immediately recognisable as Justine's child.

Rosie bore no resemblance to her father, and it was as if Paul had not made any contribution to her creation. He tried to avoid the infant, insisting that she keep away from him, as she distracted him from his work.

Justine hired a nurse, which was hardly necessary, as she spent a lot of time with little Rosie.

Mrs Diggery had never met a more committed mother, and for all the town gossip, she found Justine to be a good person.

The young woman had few complaints about her woeful lot in her loveless marriage, and a complete lack of airs or graces. The nurse observed the tension between the couple and although the reverend appeared to be the epitome of a proud father in public, his behaviour at home showed he was a sullen, cruel man.

Mrs Diggery was a sensitive woman, and she realised that little Rosie would grow up to be subtly and deliberately broken by her father if his nastiness continued unchecked. She decided to do her best to keep the baby away from the miserable man.

It was not yet three weeks after Rosie's birth that Paul Smithers insisted on having relations with his wife. Justine was still recovering, but he revolted her by making her perform particular acts to his satisfaction. Justine was still on her knees in front of her husband, when he grabbed her jaw and jerked her head upward to look at him.

"I want you pregnant again."

This time, Justine found her voice.

"It has hardly been three weeks," said Justine. "It's too soon.

"I do not care. Tomorrow, we will begin working on it," he sneered. "I want a son, and then another one until you all are used up. Hopefully, one of the births will be problematic and rid me of you for good."

She remembered her father's words that she could return to his house, but this time there would be a sacrifice involved—her beloved Rosie.

Night after night, Paul Smithers raped his wife, sometimes two or three times. She refused to give him the satisfaction of crying out, because the one time that she had, it had aroused him so much that he'd repeated the act for the pleasure of hearing her in scream all over again.

Paul's knee deteriorated increasingly, and his pain was so excruciating at times that the doctor had prescribed opium for him. The more pain he suffered, the more he tortured his wife.

Within two months, Justine was pregnant again. It was too soon after the birth of Rosie, and this time she was constantly sick, her body was exhausted. Mrs Diggery was a godsend and had it not been for her kindness, Justine would've collapsed out of despair. Little Rosie was growing into a delightfully happy child, and she lifted Justine's mood during her darker hours.

Justine was suffering another night of humiliation. She felt her husband shudder behind her, satisfied.

"Look at me!" he commanded her.

Justine turned around to look at him, wondering what his next demand would be.

"I have been transferred to England."

Justine was filled with relief. It'd mean that she could spend time alone while he travelled ahead. I *can have my baby in peace, under my father's roof.* She dared not voice her thoughts. Besides, any chance of her wants and needs being met would be obliterated once more.

"As you have proved yourself to be untrustworthy, you'll leave with me. That way, you will have no opportunity to run around with other men."

Justine didn't answer.

"There is a hospital that can perform surgery that may improve my knee. It's experimental, but I am confident it'll ease the pain I suffer."

"Good," said Justine, ambiguously.

"But where will we live? Does the bishop approve?"

"Of course, it was his suggestion. He is tremendously pleased by how I have grown the congregation here. The number of new converts exceeds that of the Catholic parish. And for the first time in years, the books are showing a profit for the region. We'll be living in the mansion next to St. Luke's Cathedral in the city.

"A mansion?" asked Justine.

"Yes, I will also get a new title," he said, haughtily.

"What title will that be?"

"Bishop of Salford, a parish much in need of support. The archbishop believes that a post in a city will alleviate the day-to-day challenges of country walking. He has great empathy for my condition, my crippled leg," sneered Paul.

"When will we leave here?"

"By the end of the month."

Justine waited until Paul was away visiting parishioners in the countryside. The weather was treacherous, but she was undeterred. She walked to the Catholic Church. Nobody paid attention to the hunched-up woman scurrying along with the shawl over her head. By the time she reached the confessional, she was rain-soaked, and her body was freezing.

Father William opened the screen.

"Justine!" he exclaimed when he saw her. "You must be freezing! let us get out of this box and go and have some tea next to the fire in my office. "C'mon, you are going to catch yer death out here child."

His kindness brought tears to her eyes, and she wiped them away before she left the confessional, preferring to give him a brave beaming smile as she opened the door.

William and Justine sat comfortably in front of the fire.

"What brings you here, Justine?"

"Paul mentioned something about a promotion to become a bishop and seeing a surgeon about fixing his knee. It'll mean a transfer to England."

"I see," William smiled.

He was so fond of the lovely girl in front of him. She was different than before. She did not look defeated, but rather discouraged.

"Whereabouts will you live then?" asked William.

"Somewhere in Greater Manchester."

William smiled wryly at her with genuine delight.

"Oh, William, stop being such a romantic. I am pregnant again. Those dreams are in the past. My focus is on my children now."

"And are you focusing on your husband?"

Justine shrugged dismissively and the conversation came to a halt.

"—Father William, is Michael still there?"

"I haven't heard from him in quite a while."

"I just wondered," she said softly.

"Once you know more, leave your new address with me, Justine, if I hear anything, I will let you know."

"Thank you, William."

"Bless you, Justine, I know that this is not what I am supposed to say—but you and Michael are meant to be together."

"I have children now."

"He will love them like his own."

"How can you be so sure?"

"Because he loves you, Justine. He does not even consider Paul an entity in your life. For Michael, your husband is just an inconvenience. I know in my bones he would've you with ten children if he could. Michael has a big heart with enough space for all of you."

16

APPOINTED A BISHOP

Justine gave birth to her second daughter thirteen months after Rosie was born. It was a smooth delivery, and the midwife was excellent. Her husband, Bishop Paul Smithers, was taken care of by his new friends, and he was away for the day and most of the night. Justine rejoiced that he was absent.

Paul arrived home in the early hours of the morning. He was drunk and aggressive. Justine didn't know where he'd been drinking or with whom, and she didn't care.

He waddled and stomped to her bedside and took the baby out of her arms. He ripped the swaddling blankets open and lifted the child into the cold air, causing the little thing to scream.

"Typical. Another disappointment, Justine," he slurred.

Justine didn't argue, terrified that he would hurt the baby.

He knew that Justine could not stand up and contest him, and he took full advantage of her weakened situation.

> "Justine, we will just have to keep trying until you give me a son. We'll begin again soon. I do not want to wait too long."

He shoved the screaming child back into her arms, then stormed off in search of more drink.

*

Mrs Diggery found Justine hysterical.

> "Now, now, Justine. Calm down. Tell me what happened?"
>
> "He is going to kill baby Hope. He is drunk and angry he doesn't have a son. I am sure he's going to kill her."
>
> "Calm down, lass. Here, here," soothed Mrs Diggery and put her arm around Justine.
>
> "I promise that I will never leave the baby alone with him, alright? And if you are afraid for yourself, call me."

Justine began to calm down.

Paul had consented to Mrs Diggery accompanying them to Manchester, so that Rosie would not demand more of Justine's time than strictly necessary. Keen that she could not nurture the children, he was delighted both mother and daughters could be punished with one of his edicts.

> "It's far easier having control over you when the children are happy. I am an important man in religious circles now, and you will play an active role in my career."

Justine shook her head at him.

> "You're not a politician Paul, you are a bishop of the Church of England," she challenged him.

> "The same, my dear, the same," he answered arrogantly.

Justine never anticipated how extreme the change in their lifestyle would be, and she learnt that a high clerical position in the church had many social demands. Thankfully, the majority of these were only for clergymen which meant that her husband spent a lot of time away from home. Only occasionally did Justine accompany him to dinner or a charitable function. The space away from her brute of a husband was welcome.

Nobody could deny that the bishop's wife was beautiful, even glamorous. Mercifully, Justine's only real public commitment was to make sure that she was at Sunday services with a smile on her lovely face, accompanied by her two dark-haired daughters.

Paul's frequent journeys and meetings distracted him so much that he left her alone and seldom made any sexual advances toward her. She prayed that he'd found a mistress. Justine was satisfied to remain in her husband's shadow. She would act the part of a happy wife and find joy in her children.

Justine and Mrs Diggery became allies, and the woman looked after Justine in the same way that she cared for the two little girls. She worked hard to create a warm, loving environment for Justine, because she knew that Justine had no friends who she could trust in the cold, marble-floored mansion.

Justine attended her first social event with Paul, who gave his wife a firm warning about scandalous behaviour.

> "At this level of society, we are required to have our house in order. That is you, my dear, as well as your two daughters."

Paul never referred to them as his children, but always as Justine's daughters. It made for witless parlour remarks, but it was true, they were Justine's.

> "I expect you to remain reserved and modest during the evening. Only speak when you are asked a direct question. I want none of your opinions or any talk of art. You'll have no interaction with any of my male colleagues. Do you understand?"
>
> "Of course," she replied.

> "I want you humble and pious. Not the jezebel I know you to be. Just remember that everybody knows your secret past even if they do not raise the matter with you."

Justine dressed modestly, but when she entered the large reception hall, to the ire of Bishop Paul Smithers, everybody turned around to look at the beautiful woman entering the room. Justine had her hair scraped from her face in a harsh style, not like the feminine floaty ringlets that were fashionable at the time. Her emerald green dress was devoid of any trimmings. Her ankles and wrists were covered up, and the collar covered her neck, touching her jawline. Still, the severity of the cut of dress accentuated her natural beauty. Her dark hair contrasted with the emerald-coloured clothing. She wore no jewellery. She didn't need to. Her black eyes sparkled more brightly than any of the gems that the other women wore.

Smithers stood stunned as he watched his colleagues study his wife. He was livid, as if she was responsible for their reaction to her. He looked at her. She'd followed his instructions, and there was nothing seductive about her attire. If anything, on a clothes hanger It'd look positively dowdy. She, herself, was beautiful, and there was nothing that he could do about it. He did have feature that he could manipulate. He snarled in her ear to stop smiling.

She followed her husband around the room, where she got introduced to countless clergymen, aristocrats, and gentry whom she would never remember.

The last introduction was the most important, as he was a very powerful man in the area.

"Archbishop Donkin, please meet my wife, Mrs Smithers."

Justine made a small curtsy while the archbishop took in every detail of the beautiful woman before him.

He took her hand in his, squeezing it a little too intimately in Justine's opinion. She was glad Paul did not pick up on the gesture. He was too preoccupied wondered how to flatter the bishop for his own benefit.

"Welcome to Manchester, Mrs Smithers. I hope that you are happy here. Your husband can be very proud of you." he said, still grasping her hand.

"Thank you, Archbishop Donkin," she replied without looking into his eyes.

"My wife will be extending a dinner invitation to you both, and it'll be a pleasure to have you visit," Donkin informed her.

"Thank you," Justine said demurely, devoid of any hint of a smile.

Paul Smithers' pretty caged songbird had played the part of a submissive wife to perfection. But while she'd suppressed her vibrant personality, she'd not suppressed her inquisitive and focused mind. She could still study people, and while she was playing her role, she was making mental notes of the characters before her and how they interacted.

Of all the guests in attendance, the person who unsettled her the most was Archbishop Donkin. He was charming, almost flirtatious and her instincts with his gestures earlier told her that he was a ruthless man, who got his way irrespective of the cost to others.

A week later, Justine and Paul received an official invitation to dinner at the home of Archbishop Donkin and his wife, Patricia. The invitation didn't daunt Justine. In fact, Paul had done her a great favour in telling her to shut up and keep to herself. She was under no social pressure to perform, and could observe all the more closely.

She put on a dark blue dress that hid all her curves, scraped her hair off her face and tried to look as drab as she could. She practised looking miserable in front of Mrs Diggery, which had the two women howling with laughter, and had the rest of the house staff wondering why she could be so happy in such a loveless home.

The Smither' coach stopped in front of an impressive detached townhouse. There were oil lamps set out along the driveway that led to the enormous dwelling, and a smartly dressed butler welcomed them as soon as he heard the wheels crunch along the driveway gravel.

The event was to be a small reception for twenty-four people. Patricia must have been doing it for years as the routine was like clockwork. Smithers revealed another edict for his browbeaten wife.

> "Take some lessons, Justine, soon you will have to do this. We'll be entertaining regularly from now on."

Justine smiled. She wished that her father was there to hear Paul. Justine came from a wealthy landed Irish family, and Paul came from much humbler stock but he still thought that he could teach her etiquette.

The first important encounter was with Lady Sedgefield, a tiny little thing who chattered like a nervous child and was clearly in love with the centre of her universe—her spouse.

The archbishop made sure that he was seen to be a doting husband. Justine hardly smiled the whole evening. Patricia Donkin was worried that her guest was unwell and took her aside.

> "My dear, are you feeling ill? I see that you are very quiet this evening."
>
> "I am fine, thank you, just a little tired by the move. It has been strenuous, and we are still getting used to the change," she lied.

The archbishop was fascinated with Justine, and he tried very hard to get her attention.

> "How did you meet such a lovely young woman?" he asked Paul in front of Justine.

Justine had little time for forward older men. The archbishop's small talk continued.

"What was your maiden name, Mrs Smithers?"

"O'Leary," answered Justine with her Irish lilt to her voice.

"I have heard of Douglas O'Leary. Are you related to him?"

"He is my father."

"By God, Smithers, the O'Leary's are almost Irish aristocracy. You have chosen very well," he said to Paul.

Paul smiled from ear to ear. He was already planning how to spend his wife's inheritance.

Justine had endured as much polite chit-chat as she could manage and excused herself to get some air. She slid away, looking for a quiet place to escape to within the house. She'd never been surrounded by such opulence and pomp in her life. Her father had no high ideas of who he was, his feet were firmly on the ground. Choosing an ideal spot, the lonely woman stood at a large bay window in the library and stared into the darkness, wishing she could leave.

Her reverie was broken when she heard the large door swing shut behind her followed by the click of a lock. As her eyes adjusted to the dark, she turned to see it wasn't her husband approaching, but Lord Sedgefield. He reached her and stood as close to he as he could get.

"Ah, Justine O'Leary. I know all about you," he
whispered in the dark.

She could feel his breath against his cheek. Justine wasn't a woman who panicked at the first sign of trouble. She turned away and walked toward the door.

She tried the handle, but the door wouldn't budge. She turned around and watched Lord Sedgefield pace toward her once more. He pushed himself up against her and pinned her to the door. His hands came up, and he started to fondle her.

"You're infamous, Justine. We all know that you
are available. How can I please you? I do not
think your husband can give you what I can."

Justine had grown up with five Irish brothers, and they knew how to fight dirty. She'd learnt from the best.

Losing her temper, she could feel the fury well up in her chest, but she didn't make a sound. The fool began to pull up her dress, and she felt his hands travel up her legs.

It was the moment she'd awaited. His hands were preoccupied, and he thought that he was in control of the situation. Justine gently pushed him back with a smile. He interpreted it as a promise, but he was wrong. Justine lifted her exposed leg and kneed him in the groin twice, as viciously as she could.

Lord Sedgefield collapsed in agony. He could not straighten himself up, and he writhed uncontrollably on the ground, groaning loudly.

Justine bent over and whispered in his ear.

"Take a good look at my husband's knee, Lord Sedgefield. I did that. If you ever touch me again, I will break both your legs."

Even through his pain, he registered what she said and nodded. He'd never heard a woman speak in such a way before, and he wasn't sure which upset him most—the pain or the menace in her quiet voice.

"Give me the key," she instructed.

He put his hand in his pocket and held it up for her to take.

"Thank you."

He knew that he would never make the mistake of fondling Justine O'Leary again.

Lord Sedgefield returned to the party half an hour later looking very pale.

"Oh my!" said the archbishop, "You look a little off, are you alright?"

"Of course, I am," sneered Sedgefield. "There is nothing wrong with me."

Justine watched Lord Sedgefield walk toward his wife with a smile, delighted that he was limping ever so slightly.

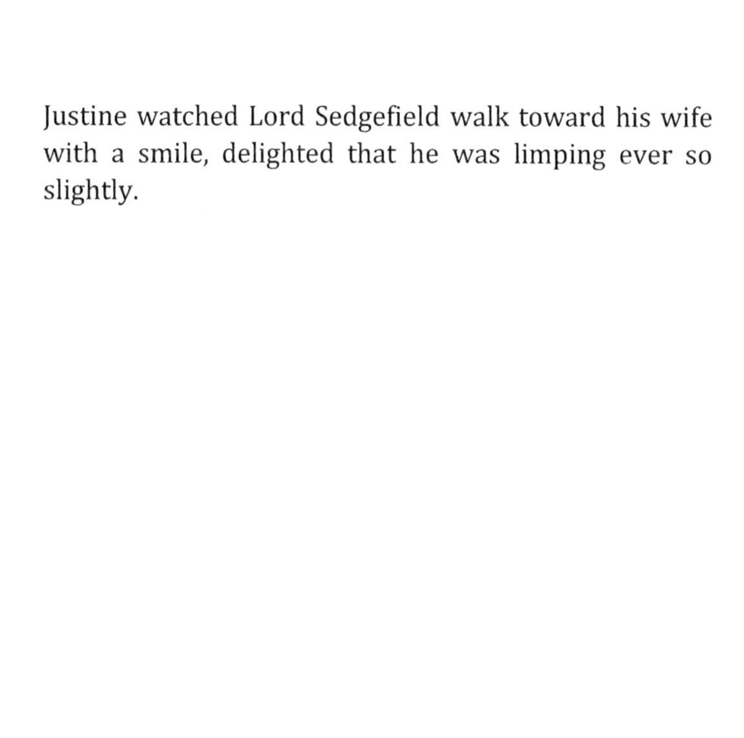

17

MICHAEL'S BOYS

The children in Mr O'Neil's class began referring to themselves as 'Michael's Boys'. They differed in age, temperament, and skill. The only thing they'd in common was Angel Meadow, the terrifying area of Manchester where they saw and experienced things that matured them way beyond their tender years.

Michael observed that the orphans who lived on the premises were more submissive than the children he saw living on the streets. Michael attributed it to the discipline and routine that would be lacking in typical slum lodging houses.

On his first day, he'd won his pupils' respect by ejecting Peter and his thugs from the classroom. Thanks to his impressive bulk, the lads preferred not to play up, thus Michael's easy-going, non-aggressive manner slowly began to endear him to them.

He loved to teach them practical—not academic knowledge and skills. The soft subjects of reading and writing were left to Mr Conrad and Mr Joyce. They'd a struggle controlling the little blighters who had no interest whatsoever in any form of classic literature or scrawling the same letter in chalk over and over again on a slate.

The teachers often asked Michael how he succeeded in bringing them to order, but he would laugh and shrug his shoulders, saying that he was just lucky.

He studied the boys in his classroom. *How many of these children will see old age?* They already looked like little old men, hunched and worldly-wise. They smoked their pipes and ciggies, while having adult conversations.

Yet, Michael identified a vulnerability as well, for all their worldly ways, they wanted attention and acceptance. They craved normalcy. As orphans, they wanted to 'belong' to someone and for that person to take pride in them.

It was a natural choice for Michael to encourage them to play football in the schoolyard on Sunday afternoons, much to the annoyance of the school board, who complained that It'd attract rabble-rousing spectators. Still, the boys loved it, especially the boarders who lived in the darkness of the attic with little stimulation other than work and study.

Michael had learnt that Peter and his scuttler friends were gang members who specialised in varying degrees of crime, from petty theft to murder. O'Neil sensed that the other lads were more relaxed when he was present. Michael's instincts told him that Mr Hayes ruled the attic with an iron fist which troubled him. As an orphan he'd been raised by good men, and he understood the value of paternal kindness in a young lad's upbringing.

As he became more familiar with the pupils and staff, he found himself becoming suspicious of Mr Hayes. He could not put his finger on what made him feel so uncomfortable around the man, still he felt his hackles rise every time he was in his presence.

Michael noted that Mr Burbidge never influenced what happened in the school, apart from being miserly with coal for the fires, perhaps. He was a mere figurehead who arrived at seven o'clock every morning and left at five o'clock, unless there was a meeting. Other than that, he hid away in his office pretending to be dealing with administrative tasks. He seemed to have little knowledge of what happened on the premises after hours.

Michael had seen the other members of the school council, but he was not introduced to them. The men would arrive in fancy carriages, with their fancy clothes and hats, but visiting teachers were far below their status. Bishop Donkin almost always accompanied them.

One staff member who captured Michael's attention was Eliza, the kitchen maid. She was a lovely, soft girl, and they got along famously, mainly because they shared strong Irish roots. They would regularly have a cup of tea together, discussing the old country and having a good natter in their Irish brogue. Often, Grant and Harry joined them, and soon the four of them became firm friends.

Eliza was in the perfect position to hear all the gossip that the servants were exposed to, and so their lives became entwined. An unshakeable trust developed between them all.

Michael refused to tolerate bullying in his classroom, and on a few occasions, he'd grabbed boys by the scruff of their necks, pulled them out of the lesson. He threatened them with bodily harm if the news ever reached his ear of them hurting another boy in his care. They knew that Michael was serious because they'd seen him physically throw the strongest challenger, Peter, out of the classroom earlier in the term.

Slowly, his pupils became more interested in their subject, and Michael's rich engineering knowledge and skills gained their respect. As Michael performed miracles with wheels, gears, pulleys, and weights, they paid more attention. They built small mechanical engines and experimented with new-fangled phenomena in the fields of electricity and chemistry. For his young wards, Michael was a magician who created his magic with machines.

He would remove his coat, roll up his shirt sleeves and gleefully get his hands dirty. The boys would crowd around him, fascinated as he explained mechanical processes to them. Occasionally, their experiments would fail, or something would blow up, which usually had them diving under their desks in fits of laughter. Still, everybody got an opportunity to show off their skills and talents, which increased their confidence in themselves tremendously.

All of a sudden, boys were going off to work, demonstrating better skills than their supervisors, solving problems that the older men could not. Michael would often visit the men who employed his pupils to understand their businesses and get better insight into what skills he could teach the youngsters that would add value in the factories where the lads worked. In his own way, Michael succeeded in satisfying master and slave.

A lot of the businessmen he consulted gave him more insight into the lives of their young workers than they would ever reveal at school. Most of the stories were heart-breaking, and most of the misery pivoted around poverty, alcohol, and disease. All that Michael could do was inspire and educate the current batch of thirty young souls for whom he was responsible.

Soon his teaching methods gained popularity, and the drab-looking school in Corning Street turned around from a place of shame to a place of hope.

Yet, not everybody was satisfied with the changes. The school board complained that the boys were far too familiar with the teachers, seeing them more as equals than leaders, and that the pupils required more discipline. The last complaint was from Archbishop Donkin, who said that the orphans who lived in the attic were getting false hope that they could rise above their stations. He argued their false sense of entitlement would wreak havoc in the workplace when their dream opportunities failed to appear.

Michael was furious when the odious archbishop dared to utter the words to his face.

> "How dare you predict their future. We are the only people that they have to give them hope. I refuse to tell them that they have no future beyond this Godforsaken hell hole called Angel Meadow."

> "You're continually testing my patience, Mr O'Neil," said Donkin arrogantly. "You're the troublesome thorn in my side."

> "Then you need to redefine the school's objectives. If you have the boys here with the very purpose of sending them into the world as cheap labour to your industrial benefactors, then you may as well shut this school. There are already a glut of establishments providing a paltry level of education. I suggest you appreciate the good work we are doing here and take some pride in the children you send out into the world."

Lord Sedgefield looked at Michael with disdain.

"The only reason that you have not been dismissed from your post is that it'll cause a commotion between our religious denominations. You may no longer be a priest, but you are still a Catholic."

Of all the children that Michael taught, there was one boy that he couldn't reach out to, no matter how hard he tried.

Young Nel was ten years old. He was a confrontational and angry soul. Nel had no friends. He never participated in anything—and he was highly aggressive. Michael hoped to entice Nel to play football with the others, but he refused. The little lad never spoke, he simply stood on the side-lines of life, mute and furious. Mr Hayes had made it clear that Nel was a problem, and that no amount of severe beatings had succeeded in reforming his rebellious outlook and insolent behaviour.

Michael was disgusted with Mr Hayes' brutal approach with the boys. He felt that the children in the area were already severely treated at home and that school should be a haven, a place where they were safe. The more resistance Nel showed, the more Michael wanted to help him.

Michael took up the subject with his colleagues.

"No, matter how I cajole him, I never receive a positive response," said Michael.

"Yes, he is sullen and obstinate. He causes scene after scene in my classroom," said Grant Conrad.

"What do we know about his background?" asked Michael.

"He is an orphan like all the others. He has a little brother called Jono. Hayes told us that Jono was sent to an aunt or perhaps someone else in the family."

"I suppose he might miss his brother? Should we find out where his family is?" pondered Michael.

"There are thousands of children like Nel, Michael. You cannot fix all of them. Put your efforts into the ones you can nurture, not those determined to sabotage themselves regardless."

"Nel is in my care for most of the day, and it's my responsibility to see to his welfare. Since he lives here, who else has he got?"

Grant and Harry could not look Michael in the eye. They were too ashamed of themselves.

"Do not ask me for help," put in Harry Joyce. "I have given up. The other day he called me an old git. I mean, imagine that from a ten-year-old."

Michael put his head back and looked at the ceiling, then started laughing at the lad's tenacity. "That news makes me want to help the little upstart all the more."

18

THE VISITORS

Michael was woken up by a sound far below him in the courtyard. He sat up alert and identified the faint sound of carriage wheels crossing the courtyard cobbles. The noise was barely audible above the wind. He lit his lamp and reached for his watch. *Two-thirty in the morning! Who can that be?* He lay in bed, straining his ears to learn more from the sounds down below, curious to know who was arriving at this odd hour. Even if he stood on his desk, he could not reach the window. 'Blasted cell,' he cursed silently as he tried to get back to sleep.

*

It was late afternoon, and it was as dark as night outside as another school day ended. Michael stepped into the courtyard warmly dressed against the weather, but the wind was soon whipping his coat around him, and he was having difficulty keeping his hat on.

Michael enjoyed teaching more than he'd expected, despite the exhaustion of being a protector and inspiring role model for the boys. This week in particular had drained him of all energy, and he looked forward to meeting Harry and Grant at the pub to have a few pints.

As he crossed the schoolyard and began walking toward the gate, he heard a shout.

"Oi, Priest!" the voice called out.

At first, Michael didn't know who it was, so he walked toward the voice and the red tip of a cigarette glowing in the dark to find out more.

"Where yer **goin**', Priest?" asked a voice.

"Depends on who's asking," replied Michael.

He got closer to the voice and was surprised to see that it was Nel hiding in the shadows.

"Good grief!" Michael exclaimed, "What yer doing out in this hooley? Surely you want to get inside and get some warmth?"

"Can I come wiv yer?" Nel asked.

"What?"

"Can I come wiv yer? I don't wanna stay 'ere by mesel', Sir."

This wasn't what Michael had planned for his relaxing evening, and he was about to fob the child off when he realised that it was an unique opportunity to meet the real Nel. Needing to choose between the pub and the lad, without a second thought the matter was settled—he decided to take Nel out for tea.

"You wait for me here, Nel, and I will tell Mr Hayes you are coming with me. He won't take kindly to you absconding, I expect."

Nel didn't answer Michael. He watched his teacher walk off with the distrusting eyes of a child who had experienced too many broken promises from adults.

"Michael, I strongly advise against taking that boy off the school premises. He will only be trouble. We have considered putting him in a mental asylum. He is a little liar with a bad mouth. The more I thrash him, the more insolent the little bugger becomes."

"Perhaps when you stop thrashing him, Mr Hayes, you may have a different result."

Hayes' eyelids flickered downwards as he let out a long dismissive sigh, then his thin mouth drooped, which caused it to disappear into the folds of his saggy jowls. For an instant, Michael caught a glimpse of the real man that lay behind the over-friendly hostel master front. *He's an actor, adept at keeping up a façade of cheer in an attempt appear harmless. But he isn't harmless or friendly. He is a tyrant.*

"Where are you taking him?" demanded Hayes.

"There is a small tea shop, two streets down near the cotton mill," answered Michael.

"Beware the little horror doesn't make a run for it, and don't believes a word he says. He'll steal the sugar out of yer tea. Do not yer come running to me if he causes trouble, do yer hear me Michael O'Neil?"

Michael stepped out into the cold and was pleased to find Nel where he'd left him. Forgetting about the pints he'd been looking forward to, he nodded invitingly in the direction of the café.

"C'mon lad, let us go and have our tea then. I am hungry."

Michael put his hand on the boy's shoulder, but Nel shrugged it off and moved away.

Together, they walked through the bitter streets. Beggars and paupers accosted them as they walked under the bridges, and Michael was troubled by the violence that Nel exhibited when anyone came close to him.

They reached the gloomy little tea shop and shared a bench with some local factory workers. Michael ordered himself tea, and Nel had a cup of steaming cocoa with sugar. They both had a sweet cinnamon bun, which was a glorious treat in the cold weather.

Halfway through their visit, Nel leant over and spoke in the faintest of whispers.

"Priest, yer can't tell anybody if I speak to yer?"

"You know I am not a priest, Nel" he tutted, "but I promise that I can keep secret—cross my heart."

Nel gave Michael's reply some thought, and sighed.

"Them sods are going to thrash me if I says anyfink. Or they'll take me away," whispered Nel.

Michael looked up, startled by the child's words, convinced that Nel wanted to tell him something significant. *Who are 'they'?* Michael didn't flinch again, knowing that if he gave any clue he was eager to hear the child's revelations, the boy would clam up, and he would get nothing more out of him again.

"That swine of a bishop, he be doing most of the beatings, Priest, and 'em Scuttlers—they hold us down."

Michael took a sip of his tea and tried to stay calm.

"Donkin, he brings over 'is toff friends with 'im, 'e does."

Michael looked into the child's eyes, willing Nel to trust him.

"Sometimes, they take 'em tiny lads and never bring 'em back like. The only reason they left me alone is cos I cursed and screamed so loudly, the fecking roof almost came down like."

Nel stopped talking and spent some time concentrating on his sticky bun, and studying the people in the tea room, terrified he might have made matters worse.

"Priest," Nel said, "do ye know Donkin?"

"I have met him a few times," Michael answered truthfully.

"Did ye meet that arse Sedgefield?"

"Yes."

"Do you like 'em, Priest?"

"No, I do not," he revealed with a shake of his head.

"Them two feckin' blokes are bloody arseholes," grizzled the boy, leaving Michael to wonder who had educated Nel in his choice of language.

"That's 'ow I sees it, Priest. Those two are pally with Hayes. They're all in on it. He lets them in to use the boys, 'specially the wee ones. All as bad as each other them lot."

Michael had a full grasp of what Nel was telling him, staggered by what he heard. Nel was matter of fact about the ordeal the boys faced. There were no bragging embellishments to his story, and Michael knew that he was telling the truth.

Michael nodded encouragingly at Nel, indicating that he should carry on talking, not daring to speak in case his unburdening ended.

"And they got a special private room in the school, Priest. Them bye-blows sit there and make the wee ones do fings only for grownups like. Then those scuttlers take the wee lads away sometimes, especially if they put up a bit of a fight. Never see 'em again."

"How many men visit?"

"Lots and lots, Priest. Hayes and Donkin had a new man there the **uvver** night. A nasty little curmudgeon, had a bad limp he did."

"Nel," Michael took a deep breath, "how do you know the scuttlers take the wee children away?"

Nel stopped dead in his tracks, no longer talking and eating, his mind taking him on a journey into the past. He seemed to be in a trance, reliving something that he'd experienced first-hand. Suddenly, he remembered where he was and started talking again. His eyes flashed wide open with a revelation.

"They took me wee bruvva, Priest. Jono, we called him. He was six years old. Those old dirty fellas took him to that special room, and I never saw him again."

"Do you have any family, Nel? Do you have an aunt where Jono could be living?"

"Nah, Priest. The whole ruddy lot of 'em died of the cholera."

"Are you sure, Nel? You have to be sure."

"' Course I'm bloody sure, Priest. Lots of us there were in that room. We boys sat with me parents. We were in filth up to our ears. Everybody died, Priest, there, in front of us. Dropped dead like flies they did—except for me and Jono."

Nel didn't cry. His emotions were locked deep inside of his little tortured soul, but they still existed. Michael knew that if he didn't help the boy, his inner demons would cause him to degenerate into a short and brutal life of violence.

Michael and Nel returned better friends than when they'd set out. Alas, but understandably so, as soon as they got to the school gates, the lad became the same silent aggressive boy he usually was. Michael realised that it was Nel's way of protecting himself. Nel, however, knew he needed more—an adult that he could trust and a place where he was safe.

Michael spent the night in turmoil. He could not trust anyone with the information Nel had divulged as he was sure that, at best, Nel would clam up, and at worst, his life would be in mortal danger if his abusers found out.

Nel's disclosure left a terrible burden upon the anxious teacher. He needed an ally, somebody who would hide Nel and keep him safe enough to testify before a court. There was only person he could risk approaching—Father McDermott.

Another Friday rolled by. Nothing had changed in Angel Meadow. The wealth of the country was being built on slave labour. The slum streets were still teeming with human and animal faeces. People were still being poisoned by the filthy water they drank. The streets were congested with people who were starving to death in the middle of a prosperous industrial city on the up.

The poor lived on top of each other like squirming rats in a dark sewer, eating what they could scavenge and leaving their young to fend for themselves. The graveyards were so full that when it rained the wooden coffins swelled in the damp, lifting them of the earth supposed to entomb them. Children loved to use them as obstacles to navigate when they played a game of 'tig'.

When Michael had thought that Angel Meadow couldn't get worse, it did. Now, men in positions of responsibility were molesting, imprisoning—perhaps even murdering—the children in their care.

A darkness settled over him, and it threatened to engulf him. Again, he was filled with dread at what was to come. Challenging these evil men would put him in terrible danger. He was desperate to go back home to the dull and predictable Bunratty parish. Resolving the forty-year rancorous O'Leary and Mulroney feud paled in comparison.

Worst of all, yet again, there was nobody to comfort him with his silent burden. His thoughts drifted to Justine, and he felt himself longing for her, which only made his woes worse.

It was Friday yet again, and another week had passed in a blur.

"Hayes," said Michael, "Nel is coming with me. We are going to tea."

Since Michael had started taking Nel out, Hayes had lost all of his charm.

"So, you've taken a fancy to the little eejit, have you?" Hayes taunted, sarcastically.

"Not the kind of fancy you are insinuating, if that is your game."

Hayes blushed with guilt. Michael wanted to kick him hard in the privates, and the thought was sweet. He promised himself that at the first opportunity he would.

Michael took his usual route across the schoolyard and met Nel at the gate, the wayward youngster calling out his usual greeting.

"Hey, Priest!"

They walked to the tea shop and found a table for themselves. Michael prayed that Nel would trust him enough to go with his plan—it was the only one he had. They ordered their tasty treats, and as usual, Nel inspected his food and only spoke when he chose to. Michael had a sense that the clock was ticking. The days were breezing by and that meant that each night, more boys were being terrorised. He'd no option but to be brave and convince Nel to agree to his scheme.

"Nel," asked Michael gently, "I have a question."

"Yeah?"

"Would you be brave enough to save the other boys from Donkin and Sedgefield, if you could?"

"'Course, Priest."

"I can take you to a safe place, where nobody can hurt you. Will you tell the court what you saw?"

"Dunno about that, Priest. They've got eyes and ears all over this city, even for a lad like me."

"That's why you won't be in Manchester."

Nel's eyes narrowed, the distrust threatening to suffocate any progress Michael had hoped for.

"I want to take you to Liverpool and hide you at a friend's house until I can get all of this sorted out."

Nel kept quiet.

"Another cocoa and a sticky bun while you think about it?"

The boy nodded. Even when the sweet snacks arrived, for thirty minutes sat in utter defiance, Nel said nothing. It was clear to Michael knew that neither cajoling or forcing the lad to respond would work.

"Where will you take me?"

"To my friend."

"Is he a priest like you?"

"He is better."

"Really!"

"Yes, my boy, really."

Nel nodded his serious little head.

"Yes, Priest, I tell on 'em in court—but you better promise me on your life you won't let me down. I'll be a goner if they get hold of me first, you hear me?"

"I promise, Nel," replied Michael with all the solemnity he could muster.

*

Michael and Nel boarded the last train to Liverpool. They were both exhausted. In an unexpected show of trust, Nel fell asleep against Michael's arm. There was no chance of sleep for Michael. He'd never felt so afraid, or so lonely in all his life.

This time, he was the rescuer, and Nel was the child on the side of the road. It was not the confrontation in court that Michael feared, but the responsibility. He held the fate of many children's lives in his hands, not just Nel's.

Father McDermott answered the banging door, and the moment he saw Michael, once more his jovial rotund body jiggled with laughter. Nel peeked around him and formed an opinion of the cleric at the entrance.

"Who's this fat fella—Friar Tuck?"

Michael winced, then gave a nervous smile to his colleague.

"Come in! Come in, what time of the night is this to visit? Are you sober?"

"Unfortunately, I am," confessed a laughing Michael.

Mrs Bunting appeared, as if sent, and Michael greeted her.

"My word Michael, this must be important. Can I make some tea?" she asked.

"Do you have something stronger?" giggled McDermott, "I reckon the chap needs it."

Father McDermott started chuckling again. His cheerfulness was contagious, and the black cloud that hung over Michael lifted as if by magic.

"Please can we put the boy in a bed?" Michael asked the Mrs Bunting. "He is dead on his feet."

"Has he eaten?" she asked.

Nel nodded his head. The strict and matron-like Mrs Bunting looked the shabby urchin up and down as if he was a dirty window needing a damn good clean.

"Tomorrow, you will wash and scrub yourself—that is if you want to sleep in between my clean sheets," she cautioned him.

"Yes, Ma'am," he answered in a flash.

Michael almost collapsed in shock. That reply the closest Nel had ever come to exhibiting any form of respect.

When they were sure the lad was settled, Michael and Father McDermott became earnest.

"Michael, if you leave Nel here, I promise you that nobody will find him or hurt him. We'll keep him safe. I can even summons some Jesuits to guard him if necessary. They have got an excellent reputation as far as violence goes."

The man's round body jiggled again, which made Michael laugh with him. After two glasses of Father McDermott's best scotch, Michael finally relaxed. He was relieved to be sat in front of the warm fire, in a safe, comfortable house with a friend whom he could trust.

"Father, I do not want to draw the church into a scandal. The fact that it involves our spiritual opposition can be catastrophic."

"You're the voice of those children, Michael. It's your duty to speak for them. I find all people do terrible things, irrespective of what religion they are."

Michael nodded.

"You were sent here to do penance, Michael."

"Indeed, I was," he replied.

"Was she worth it?" asked Father McDermott. "You have such a strong work ethic it can't be laziness that got you into trouble."

Michael was taken aback.

"She? What are driving at, Father?"

"The woman you fell in love with, Michael—was she worth it?"

Michael didn't have to think very long.

"She was worth every moment," he confessed. "—Every moment."

Michael returned to the school on the first Sunday morning train, leaving Nel in the care of Father McDermott. When Hayes spotted his nemesis in the dining room, he rushed over with an anxious look on his fat pasty face.

"Where is Nel?" demanded Hayes.

"I don't know. I am not his keeper."

Hayes bent over menacingly and placed his fat hand on the dining table.

"He went out with you on Friday. Today is Sunday. Where is he?" Hayes growled in Michael's ear.

"I bought him tea, and sent him on his way. I was off to meet Grant and Harry in the pub as usual, so there was no need for me to return with him," Michael replied casually.

"And where the hell were you on Friday and Saturday night?"

Michael gave a smug grin, desperate to throw Hayes off the scent.

"I've was with my woman—but that's none of your business."

"Did you take Nel with you?"

"Of course, not! Who would do something like that? Young eyes should be protected from that sort of thing."

Michael tilted his head to one side and stared at Hayes. Hayes feigned embarrassment at the salacious talk.

"Look, Hayes. It's very simple. We went for tea near the cotton mill, then I told the boy to get back here before lights out, or woe betide him. Don't tell me the little bugger ran away? I genuinely thought I was making some progress reforming the, lad."

Hayes was furious.

"I told you he would be trouble—not to trust him. Now you can see why! He has caused endless trouble for me. The members of the school board want him gone. His disruptive rants and curses are unbearable. He is already displaying all the signs of a lunatic."

"Does Nel have a family?" Michael asked, playing dumb. "Any older brothers or sisters who might put him up? He's probably gone there—given up on schooling. As you say, he is hardly an intellectual. I doubt he is afraid of a school inspector taking him to task about truancy. Earning a bit of cash at on the black market would appeal to him."

Hayes looked uncomfortable. Michael sensed what he said next was bound to be a lie.

"Lord Sedgefield told me that he has an aunt. She took in his little brother Jono to her."

"Perhaps that's where—you—should begin—your—search for Nel," taunted Michael. "Unless you want me to pay her a visit?"

Hayes became flustered and declined the offer.

"Well, Mr Hayes, it seems the boy has run away," Michael said throwing his hands up in the air in defeat. "There is nothing I can do about it."

"I had better get Peter and the boys searching for him **in case** he decided to go on a little adventure on his own. He could be anywhere in the rows or living on the street. They boys will smoke him out of his hidey hole if he's around here."

"Let's hope so," said Michael, feigning concern.

He clenched his fists in contempt as he watched Hayes walk away. Thankfully, Michael, at least, had the satisfaction of knowing that Nel's whereabouts and that he was safe.

19

THEY MEET AGAIN

Ever keen to impress around the diocese, Bishop Smithers insisted that his wife Justine accompany him on a philanthropic visit.

"Archbishop Donkin has instructed that we visit a school with him. It's one of his most successful projects in the country. He is terribly proud of it. The London newspapers have been instructed to publish an article. No doubt a picture of us all will accompany the article. It's a good opportunity to raise my profile on a national scale."

"It sounds more like propaganda, not an article," Justine commented.

"Keep your opinions to yourself, Justine. Do not flatter yourself by thinking that your comments are important to anyone else."

Archbishop Donkin appeared at the school like he was the messiah descending upon the Mount of Olives. His carriage was the first to arrive at the school, and as it drew to a halt his driver flew off the seat and hastily opened the carriage door for him. The cleric was clad in a black cassock and purple paraphernalia, all indications that he was spiritual royalty.

He shook hands with everyone in the welcoming party, which included the teachers. Donkin greeted Michael as if he'd never met him before. Small bands of journalists fluttered around him like little finches waiting to pick up any tit-bit of information that the man would throw their way. Mrs Donkin alighted from the carriage and walked behind her husband. She'd a pinched little face that had not been seen a smile in years. She didn't make eye contact with any of the people with whom she spoke. When Donkin reached the top of the stairs, he'd the cheek to turn around and make the sign of the cross.

Sedgefield and the more gentrified classes arrived next. Their wives dressed fashionably, wearing huge hats with floaty plumes of ostrich feathers, all in a competition to see who could afford to have the most giant display sitting on their heads. As they accompanied their husbands, they were paraded in front of all the onlookers like trophies.

Sedgefield was silently thanking the Lord that Nel had disappeared. The wayward child was a risk at this kind of function, and he would think nothing of yelling out the men's secrets. The immediate threat of being exposed by Nel was gone with his disappearance. The question the men fretted over was where he might pop up later.

Little boys handed the snobbish wives large, expensive bouquets. The money spent on the ephemeral display of flowers could have fed a small family for a year. The wealthy entourage was standing in the middle of Angel Meadow. They could see what dismal conditions people lived in, and still, they accepted the flowers with a sense of entitlement. It seemed they thought to hell with those who had to make the sacrifices.

An unadorned coach arrived, and a plain woman got out of the cab. She stood entirely apart from the other visitors and made no social effort to greet any of the attendees. She didn't acknowledge the pupils or accept bouquets. The obligatory big fashionable feathery hat was absent from her head, preferring something more understated. She'd black hair and green eyes. The only jewellery she wore was a large emerald that was the colour of her eyes, but her most striking feature was a long scar that ran down the side of her face, from her temple to her jaw.

Michael was too busy focusing on his pupils when the last carriage arrived. He was trying to imagine how they felt having their economic and personal oppressors so close to them in the light of day. Their fear and resentment would be significant.

The young teacher felt guilty. He should've been standing with them, showing solidarity with their plight. He began to realise why the poor hated the ruling classes, people who exploited them mentally, physically, and financially. Ultimately, these boys would've their little lives destroyed because they were trapped and nobody would help them.

Michael turned his gaze back to the latest arrival. Another doddery bishop got out of the last carriage, relying on a solid walking stick to help him along as he limped toward the steps. Michael recognised him immediately and stood aghast. It was wasn't an old man at all, but Bishop Smithers. Behind him, his wife was assisted from the carriage by a footman.

Michael felt his heart begin to thump in his chest. He didn't know what to say or do. He hated the man and the rebel in him refused to acknowledge that Paul Smithers existed. Justine was a different matter.

Smithers stood in front of Michael O'Neil and put out his hand. Michael ignored him entirely and took a step backwards forcing the bishop to move along. The snub was intentional, and he didn't care who was watching him.

Justine calmly continued to greet every teacher in the row, and when she reached Michael, she put out her hand like she'd done with everybody else. Michael took

Justine's hand in his, and they looked into each other's eyes.

"You!" she mouthed, her eyebrows racing up
her forehead in surprise.

They'd been apart for so many years, but nothing about Justine had changed apart from her dress sense. She'd been instructed to wear a dull grey dress and a plain black hat, but instead of the clothes disguising her beauty, they enhanced it. Her dark hair and peach skin were flawless, but her black eyes were lacklustre and passionless.

"Mr O'Neil," he said, offering his hand.

They looked into each other's eyes as Michael took her gloved fingers in his own. She felt them disappear into his warm and calloused palm. *Once more, I am safe in his presence.* Smithers was enraged as he observed his arch-rival speaking to his wife.

Justine struggled to keep from touching Michael while she spoke to him. A lock of her wild hair unravelled, and he was about to reach out and tuck the lock behind her ear gently, but stopped short of touching it. They tried desperately hard to downplay their emotions for each other, yet it was hopeless. After years of lonely isolation for the soul mates, clues were bound to be apparent to onlookers. Those who watched closely could see that something was happening between them. Paul Smithers was one of them.

Michael and Justine stood side by side in the great hall. Neither of them cared what her husband thought as he watched them. They discretely manoeuvred themselves so they could be out of earshot.

"You left the church?" said Justine.

"They sacked me," Michael said in a sober voice. "I had an affair with a married woman."

Justine smiled.

"How did they find out?"

"I confessed."

"Were they angry?"

"Angry that I made love to you, but very happy that I walloped your husband for calling me a eunuch. Don't tell the Bishop of Dublin I told you," he added with a smile.

"I am sorry. You lost everything, and you ended up here."

"Don't be. There has been one big benefit. I have rather enjoyed being able to cultivate my engineering side."

"So, that's what you teach—engineering?"

It was more of a statement than a question from Justine.

"Yes, for the moment. It's penance for my sins."

He smiled as he looked down and her.

"Was the sin worth the penance?"

"Of course, I would do it again, only this time I this time I would marry her."

Justine smiled and shook her head. As always, things were going too fast.

"Are you happy?" Michael asked her.

"I have two children, little girls," said Justine.

He saw her soften as she mentioned them.

"What are their names?"

"Rosie and Hope."

Michael smiled. He looked around the room and took note of the men that he saw.

"Do you know all of these men, Justine?"

"Not to talk to, but I know their names."

"When you get home, write down the names of everybody who is here today."

"Why?"

"Please do it, and post the list to me without a return address."

Justine nodded.

"I'd like to talk to them about engineering jobs for my boys. I am sure they meet lots of factory owners at the freemasons' lodge," he lied. "And, who is that woman?"

"Which one?"

"The plain-looking one with the scar."

"That is Shilling Hudson, Samuel Hudson's daughter.

"The industrialist?" asked Michael.

"Yes."

"Is she friendly with these men?"

"Not at all. They do not like her. She has a school like this in Birmingham."

"I want to see you again," said Michael, changing the subject.

Justine looked around nervously to see if anybody had heard him, but still nobody was paying attention except Paul, and he was on the other side of the room.

"I have children now."

"I understand."

"Everything is different now. My girls are my world these days. You missed your opportunity, then and forever," she said softly.

"Stop it," Michael said to her. "You sound as bitter as Paul."

"Of course, I am, you walked away! I begged you to stay," she said in reserved tones. "We both knew you were wavering in your commitment to the church."

"For God's sake," he muttered under his breath, "are you going to make me pay forever?"

"Can't you see it's time to move on," Justine said with irony. "People are watching us."

Justine watched as Michael approached Shilling Hudson. The woman was beautiful, and Justine felt a pang of jealousy as she watched him introduce himself. She watched him speak to her. He'd a natural charm and made intelligent conversation.

"I have heard that you run a school like this in Birmingham," said Michael studying the beautiful woman as he spoke.

"Yes, I do," answered Shilling.

"Do you have a board of trustees or a governing council who run it?"

"I do not believe in those," said Shilling with a smile, "I like to be in charge."

Michael's eyes travelled from her eyes to the emerald. They were a precise match.

"Do you know any of these men?" asked Michael.

"These are not my kind of people, Mr O'Neil. I rescue others from men like this."

The smile returned to his face. *Perhaps I have found a powerful ally?*

"And you are attending today because—?"

"I am opening a manufacturing facility in Manchester, and I want to invest in people like I did in Birmingham."

Michael nodded at her worthy endeavours.

"I teach the boys about the sciences, engineering in particular. May I approach you if I have any ideas?"

"Yes, please," smiled Shilling Hudson, "I will appreciate it."

"Why do you do it? Why do you invest in people?" asked Michael, curious to understand what motivated her.

"Someone invested in me Mr O'Neil, transformed my life entirely, and this is my way of repaying the debt."

Two days later, Michael received three letters.

The first one was from Shilling Hudson, giving him her contact details. He was glad to know that she was serious about the factory.

The second letter was from Father McDermott in Liverpool. He told Michael that Nel was safe. He said that he'd never met such a polite young man and that Mrs Bunting had taken him under her wing as if he were her own child. Michael couldn't help but laugh out loud. He was staggered that they were talking about the same foul-mouthed badly behaved lad that he left behind. *Well, there you go, Mr Hayes. A hooligan can be reformed without a cane.*

The third letter was from a woman called Mrs Diggery, and it was the list of names he'd asked Justine to send him. He perused the list. He didn't recognise any names except Donkin, Sedgefield, and Smithers. But he was impressed by the titles of the other men on the list—lord, baron, Sir. These were important people, all wealthy and influential, but they were also depraved crooks that preyed on the weakest of society—and he was going to prove it.

Michael found an additional, smaller sheet of paper inserted in the main letter. It wasn't signed. He assumed that it was from Justine. It was an invitation to meet its author at the botanical gardens in Manchester the next Saturday.

He sat back in his chair and looked up and contemplated the last few days. Seeing Justine was a shock. She was as beautiful as he remembered her, and as feisty. He smiled to himself. Still, she was wasting her life with Paul Smithers. She was destined to do greater things, even if that was just as a loving mother. His mind drifted to Smithers, and he remembered how he'd beaten Justine, how she'd wanted to hurt him as much as he hurt her.

Michael sat in silence for a long time. In his reverie, he suddenly remembered something that critical that Nel had said.

"The feckin' bye-blow had a limp."

Michael sat bolt upright.

"No!" he exclaimed loudly. "It cannot be."

The only man in the entourage that walked with a limp was Bishop Paul Smithers.

20

INVITATION TO LOVE AGAIN

Michael didn't have to see Justine to know that the two dark-haired little girls he'd spotted belonged to her. He saw a proud mother sitting on a bench occasionally calling after the two children to be careful. Justine's adoration for them was undeniable. It was written in every expression, every encouraging nod as she watched them run around the fountain. Justine looked soft and feminine in a simple white dress, a contrast to the harsh black dress that she'd worn to the school.

Nervously, he walked over to the bench.

"They look just like you," he noted as he took a seat. "They're beautiful."

Justine smiled and subtly touched his hand. They made no attempt to move until they saw the children running over. The two little girls threw themselves into their mother's lap, laughing, and she bundled them closer to her.

"Rosie, Hope," Justine said, "This is my friend Mr O'Neil."

"Hello Mr—Oh—," they said in unison, struggling to say his name.

Michael laughed and dropped onto his haunches to be at their level.

"Who is Rosie?" asked Michael.

"Me!" yelled the elder of the two.

"And who is Hope?"

"Me!" yelled the little one, mimicking her sister.

"I think it's the other way around," teased Michael.

"Nooooo!" they yelled together.

They were soon distracted though, and headed back to the fountain, enticed by the water, and prepared to get wet from top-to-toe if they could get away with it. Justine warned them off.

"You know you are not allowed to play in the water in winter."

"Yes, mama," they called back in harmony.

"They listen to you," said Michael.

"If I dare turn my back, they'll do as they wish," confided Justine. "They need close supervision."

"Aah, so they're like their mama," he said quietly.

"Is that good or bad?"

"It's good—very good."

They sat in silence for a while, watching the joyful children.

"Will they tell their father that I was with you?" asked Michael.

"No, he never talks to them. He never really sees them. That suits me—I prefer it that way."

Michael nodded and watched them dip their little hands in the water, thinking it was a shame they lacked a father figure in their young lives.

"Hey! What did I tell you?" Justine called out. "Go and look for fairies under the trees."

They did take their hands out of the fountain, but ran in the opposite direction of the trees. Exasperated, Justine turned her head towards Michael.

"You seem to enjoy being a part of children's lives. Have you ever thought of marrying now you are no longer a clergyman?" she asked.

"Of course, I have."

Justine felt a pang of jealousy, yet she knew that had no right to react that way. Her reticence had contributed to their shared problem.

"I met someone that I liked who works at the school, but I did not tell her how I felt. I did not want to break her heart."

"Why do you say that?" asked Justine.

"I knew that if you came back, I would leave her."

"Perhaps you should've pursued her."

"Perhaps," he said uncomfortably.

"Do you ever think of me?"

"All the time," answered Michael.

"But you do know that we can never be a couple?" Justine reminded.

Michael didn't answer her.

"He is a bishop, and he is powerful. He would make life very difficult. The authorities would always believe a man of the cloth over me. He has not been a bigamist or committed incest. He has been cruel and beaten me, but not excessively so. He was careful not to beat me around the head to hide the bruising. I would be laughed out of court. And then there's the eyewatering cost to consider."

"So, he has stopped using you as a punch bag at least?"

"Yes, thankfully. Paul doesn't even demand his conjugal rights anymore."

Michael fidgeted and moved around on the bench. He gaze fell upon the little children chasing squirrels. It was a welcome distraction. He felt uncomfortable listening to the details of Justine's intimate life with her husband.

"Since we moved here, he doesn't come near me," Justine continued. "He is hardly ever home. The archbishop is very demanding of his time. When he is in Manchester, he spends most of his time at the Archdiocese. He only gets home in the early hours of the morning, sometimes not at all. But it suits me."

"You're sure about that? Michael asked, suddenly wide-eyed as another piece of Nel's puzzle was confirmed and clicked into place.

"About what?"

"Getting home in the early hours of the morning."

"No, Michael, I can't do it. You mustn't visit me at the house. They'll take my children away. I forbid you."

"I am not asking to visit you in your posh bleedin' house, Justine," he cursed. "Is he always late in coming home? Answer me, dammit."

"Often, yes?"

"What sort of time?"

Michael shrugged, not wishing to betray Nel's confidence.

"I don't know. Mrs Diggery tells me at breakfast sometimes, if she was up tending to one of the girls in the night. My husband, and I do not share the same room anymore—not that I have to justify our arrangements to you."

"You don't have to justify anything to me. I was merely asking a question," he growled, frustrated he was unable to explain why.

Michael and Justine sat in silence for a long time. He was worried about her welfare, all the more now he'd decided Smithers had to be the man with the limp. The conversation had taken an odd turn, and Justine was confused by all the strange questions that Michael was asking her.

The young man was deep in thought. *Should I or should I not tell Justine what was happening? I trust her with my life, but I don't want to involve her in this sordid mess. What if she blurts the information out in the heat of an argument with that rogue? Or if he strikes her again, and she retaliates with words?*

/"Why are you asking all these questions?"

"I need to go," Michael said apologetically. "It's getting late."

It was still early in the day and the girls were happy playing. Justine felt disappointed their rendezvous was ending.

"Will we see each other again?" she asked, croakily.

"Of course," he said gently.

She did not get up. The impeding loneliness and isolation was about to engulf her again. She regretted being cold and brisk with him.

"Goodbye," she said.

She swallowed hard and blinked a few times to make sure the tears that were beginning to sting her eyes didn't tumble down her cheeks and give the depth of her true feelings away.

Michael didn't say goodbye. He was too choked with emotion to utter that painful word. Instead, he bent over and blew her a kiss her tenderly. Her smile warmed his heart.

"Justine," he confessed quietly, "I will love those children like my own. When I look at them, I can only see you, not him. I have loved you since I first saw you. Never forget that."

She watched him walk away and leave her behind like he'd done so many times before. Feeling dreadfully sad, she fought off the desire to cry. Her two children were running toward her, and she refused to do anything that might upset them—now or in the future.

21

THE PLOT

The dockside was crowded with sailors, porters, and general labourers all looking for day work offloading cargo. The nearby dockers pub was functional but dingy, its raw wooden benches and tables stained black from workmen's overalls. The noisy crowd was made up of men and prostitutes. A simple counter-top bar dominated one wall.

Peter's table was covered with bottles and glasses. A beer that had spilled onto the table was pooling and congealing into sticky puddles. The scuttlers were too drunk to realise that their arms and sleeves were resting in it. Flies had begun to settle the rims of their pints, and they swatted them away. An occasional rat also ran over their feet, but they were oblivious to that. Peter caught Hayes' eye and waved him over.

"Right bleedin' hole this is," grizzled Hayes.

"No, better than that bloody room at school that you 'entertain' in," peter scowled.

"Now, what is eating you, Peter? We have paid you well! It sees you right for all this beer, doesn't it?"

Peter glared at Hayes. It was time to make his concerns known to the hostel master.

"What are we going to do about O'Neil? I am not happy with the way he has snooped around the place since he arrived. The school was doing just fine until he put his bloody nose in everything. I am sure he knows something about Nel. He must do."

Hayes nodded.

"What are our options, Peter? How far are you prepared to go for the cause? You know that Sedgefield and Donkin think that you are a sterling bloke," said Hayes. "I am sure they'll reward you for going above and beyond."

Peter puffed himself up at the compliment. Hayes didn't want him overconfident. It'd lead to careless mistakes, so he decided to tone down the sycophancy a notch.

"I think that O'Neil has a sniff in the nose for what's happening after hours," Hayes warned. "We have to do something about it. We have a lucrative little business running, and we don't want to lose a good income because of his meddling."

"Me and the scuttlers can get rid of him if that's what you want," boasted Peter, proud of the fact that he wielded some decision-making power in his gang.

"Calm yourself down, lad. I want a conclusion to this, not another **flippin'** catastrophe. We'd a right job on our hands with that young lad. What was his name—? Oh yeah, Jono."

"Agreed. There were a few amateurish slip-ups—but that was quickly and easily dealt with once I realised."

Hayes nodded and took a sip of his beer.

"I want it done soon, Peter—the sooner, the better. I know nothing much about the man's movements apart from he likes a tipple on a Friday evening. He's often with his colleagues Tweedledum and Tweedledee, so you will have to be patient and choose the right place and time. Leave him in a place where nobody will care to look."

Peter started to laugh loudly.

"I know, just the place."

"Good for you, lad," **Hayes** patronised Peter. "The bonus will make it all worth it if all goes to plan."

"Pray, tell," said Peter dramatically.

"Money of course, and a little trip to London. We don't want the police on our backs, now do we? You've always said you fancy seeing the bright lights and big city. Now's your chance!"

Peter looked at him and thought for a while. His cheerful mood suddenly changed.

"I think you and your rich friends are making a fool out of me. Do you think I am stupid? I don't want to get paid for an one-off job. If I am going to help keep things quiet from the authorities, I want in on the whole operations—I want a cut of the profit."

Hayes lost his temper.

"Who the hell do you think you are lad? You're just a lackey, and we can replace you whenever we like. There are plenty like you in the back alleys of The Meadow," whispered Hayes furiously.

"You forget that I know where the bodies are, and if any information leaked out—well—I can't be responsible for what happens. Why wouldn't I squeal? It'd shorten my stretch in Strangeways if I divulged a few juicy details. I wouldn't rat on my boys, but well, I ain't got a lot of goodwill to those posh toffs."

"Is this blackmail?"

"Nothing that harsh, Hayes. It's just business. Let us start with something small. Sort me out a decent hotel in London in the West End. I am not staying in bloody Whitechapel, do you understand?"

Hayes nodded. He'd bred a monster that was coming back to bite him.

Hayes left the bar an anxious man. He'd lost control over Peter. No amount of coaxing—or threatening—would change the gang lad's mind. He might be young, but he was shrewd, and had a good idea of what the men were making out of the business. Driven by greed, he was determined to get his fair share.

*

Michael O'Neil felt as if the world had a vendetta against him. He couldn't be with the woman he loved, and he was burdened with the responsibility of exposing a group of vengeful men who feasted upon the innocence of his boys.

On Saturday night, he left a note for the headmaster saying that he'd been in agony all day and needed to consult a doctor urgently. In the morning, he woke up early and snuck out and headed towards the university. He was sure their library would've what he was looking for—legal texts. He knew nothing about the civil court processes, only ecclesiastical ones, but he did know that what was happening at the school was illegal, and he was determined the men would not wriggle off the hook with the help of their expensive QCs. He was sure a book would give him enough knowledge on how best to proceed.

His chief concern was that he couldn't trust anybody. If word got out that he was asking strange questions about influential men, he was convinced they would kill to silence him—and he was of no use to the boys if he was dead.

Even for a well-educated man, the library at the law faculty was daunting. He'd never realised that there were so many subjects relevant to studying law. History, philosophy, Latin, Greek, the topics were endless. Entirely overwhelmed, he was still too embarrassed and afraid to ask the librarian to find the books that he needed. How could he ask someone to find him a book on laws pertaining to carnality or buggery?

Instead, he asked the librarian if he could use the cataloguing system. The older man led him to an anteroom and explained how the system worked. After wasting two hours trying to find the law volumes that he was looking for, he felt frustrated and discouraged. There were umpteen titles, cross-references, subjects, acts, bills, files—but nothing that could be understood by a layman. Michael was about to give up when he heard a voice behind him.

> "'Scuse me guv. I've been watching you, I 'av, and you don't look like ye know what yer looking for," said a voice in a broad cockney accent.

Michael didn't know who the cheeky little man was or where he came from. A short skinny little fellow with hard features popped up in front of him pushing a book-laden trolley.

"Who are you?" asked Michael.

"I shelve the returned books, guv. I've worked here for years now. I kind of know me way 'round all these books and **fings**. I gave up telling the students I was just a glorified cleaner and decided to learn a bit more to help 'em instead. Made my life easier, you see? They got a bit shirty and looked down at me when I kept saying I didn't know where stuff was. I'd had a bellyful of 'em being all snooty. So, I started to fill in a few gaps in my knowledge."

"Where do you come from?" asked Michael.

"From 'em offices there in the corner where I was collecting more stuff to shelve, guv."

"No, I mean where did you live before Manchester?" he asked in clarification.

"Aw, guv! Maybe I ain't that clever after all, ha **ha**!" the man chuckled. "I am from London, the rough bit mind, the East End, not la-de-da Kensington."

"I see. And what's your name?"

"Edgar John Fields, but me friends call me Eddy."

"Well, Eddy, I am looking for information, but the subject is a little delicate," muttered Michael.

"Mmm," said Eddy, "I think I knows what sort of lively stuff yer mean guv. C'mon now, give it a name or you'll stand 'ere all the bloody day. I know more about what's on these shelves than these cards."

Michael froze.

"Look guv, yer must understand **somefink**. Laws are made to punish bad people for the bad stuff they do. They don't deal with folks forgetting to offer the vicar a cup of tea when he visits—so, pipe up. You won't shock me, mate."

Michael took a breath and told Eddy what he was looking for. Eddy didn't bat an eyelid.

"Come **wiv** me, guv."

He led Michael to a different area of the library.

"This section has **everyfink** you need, but this book 'ere, it's probably the best."

"Are you sure, Eddy?"

"Course guv, I read all 'em books when I do night shift. Offences against the Persons Act 1861 that is what yer looking for. You better get cracking if you're going to get them wrong '**uns** what they deserve. They didn't hang 'em after 1861. What a bleedin' pity me finks. "

Michael was so absorbed in his reading that he lost track of time. He was surprised when Eddy came to tell him that it was time to go.

"Did ye find what yer wanted, pal?"

"Eddy, I owe you a pint, mate. Your help was invaluable."

"Anytime guv, anytime."

After a lot of head-scratching, Michael had indeed found what he was looking for. When he reviewed the gruesome examples in case law, he was even more determined that the devils perpetrating these vicious crimes would go to jail for the rest of their lives.

"Feeling thirsty now, Eddy?" asked Michael, keen for some refreshment after a long hard day.

"You bet!" replied Eddy with a grin.

*

The two men sat at a table in a nearby pub, aptly named: 'The Britons Protection.'.

"Let me tell ye a story, guv," said Eddy. "It's strange that ye do not know it. It's from your neck of the woods, it is. Bloody vicar he was, fiddled wiv parish kids he did. He got found out and the judge gave him the death sentence.

Yeah, he was s'posed to hang from his bloody neck he was. Anyways, ye know what the swine did guv, he escaped and buggered off te Scotland, like. Conned his way into a job as a butler. Can you believe it? They only found out years later. How ain't that a frontpage news story, guv?"

Michael nodded grimly.

"Wiv the new law, they don't hang 'em anymore, they put 'em one of her Majesty's hotels for a long time. Or send 'em to some far-flung penal colony. I fink death is better meself. All 'em rich boys can't get special favours smuggled in when they're dead. Death makes everyone equal."

At the end of the evening, a grateful Michael shook Eddy's hand.

"Can I call on you again if I need help, my good man?"

"'Course, guv. What are friends for? Thanks for the pint."

"Pints—" added Michael with a friendly wink.

"You go steady now, mate."

"Aye."

Michael shook his hand then headed back to the school, relieved by what he'd learnt, but too exhausted to think any further. All he wanted was food, his bed, and if he were honest, Justine.

He navigated his way through the maze-like streets of Angel Meadow and listened to the noises coming from the rows as he passed by. The homeless lived in their dark shadowland, and it felt eerie being able to hear them, but not see them. Michael rounded the corner and saw the school building ahead of him.

*

His attackers took him by surprise from behind as he hurried past the empty plot next to the school, its awful rotting stench of faeces and foetid flesh filling the night air. Michael didn't have a chance to fight back. All he remembered was a terrible pain shoot through his skull before the darkness overcame him.

Michael drifted in and out of consciousness for a few hours until his traumatised brain allowed him to awaken. He was disoriented, and it took quite some time to find his bearings. Michael realised where he was, smelling his precise location before he saw it.

Blood ran down his face and his head was throbbing. He raised his hand and felt the wound behind his ear. Then, he tried to move his body, but his chest felt crushed. *I can't lie here until morning. They'll know I lied about the doctor. I must reach the school.*

Michael crawled out of the filth on his hands and knees. He didn't make it very far very fast because every breath felt like there was a knife piercing his lung. He'd to stop every few inches to regain his energy before he could crawl further. He felt compelled to stand up soon, even close to death he was too proud to be seen crawling into the schoolyard.

Michael forced himself as far as the school wall, lurching from shadow to shadow, steadying himself against it until he felt his dizziness subside. So, close to the finishing line, he took one step and then another, and soon he started to stumble toward the school doors faster and faster. His technique would've made an excellent lesson on momentum.

All he could do was concentrate on staying erect and one step at a time. There was still a light on in the headmaster's study. *Damn and blast! Burbidge is working late. Why tonight of all nights?* Michael opened the door and collapsed onto the floor in the entrance hall. Mr Burbidge was alarmed when he heard the front door slam. Vandals regularly defaced the school, so he got up to see if somebody was there, but by the time he reached the foyer, it was empty.

Determined that nobody would see him, Michael crawled to the rickety servants' staircase, and he reached out for the rail. Every time he moved his arms, it felt as if his chest would explode. He'd just reached the first landing when he heard light steps coming down the staircase toward him.

Kevin Finlay got the fright of his life when he fell over Michael in the dark.

"Who's that?" said Michael.

The boy recognised Michael's voice.

"It's me, sir, Kevin."

It was the boy that he'd saved from Peter early on in his appointment.

"Not a word of this to anyone, lad," Michael instructed him. "Go up and fetch Eliza, and do not wake anybody up."

Michael grunted, struggling for breath as he fought to stand once more. Moments later, Kevin came down with Eliza, dressed in her nightclothes, pulling her dressing gown tightly around her to protect her modesty. Together they dragged him to her room because he could not manage to climb another flight of stairs. Carefully they lay him on the bed, and Eliza lit the lamp.

"Oh, no!" Eliza and Kevin exclaimed simultaneously.

If Michael had felt severely injured in the dark, he looked far worse in the light.

Eliza and Kevin cleaned his head wound. He didn't know where Eliza had found bandages, but she strapped his chest firmly, and he only experienced a minimum of chest movement when he breathed. Michael's body was covered with bruises, and Eliza was surprised that he'd no broken bones. They helped him into some night clothes.

"You can stay here for the night," she told him, "I will sleep in your room. I'll come back to check on you early in the morning. I can't see you getting much sleep in all that pain."

"Thanks," said Michael.

"Who do you think did this?" she asked him.

"I would suppose it was Peter and the boys."

"Yes, it likely was. You have been kicked to pieces and those buggers wear them darned clogs with sharp metal toecaps."

"Eliza, I do not want you involved with this. No one must know I am here."

"I suppose," agreed Eliza, torn between wanting to get justice for her battered colleague and a strong sense of self-preservation.

"Same with you, Kevin. If these lads find out that you know they did this to me, you will be the next in line for a beating."

Kevin nodded, knowing all too well Michael was right.

"You need to rest now," warned Eliza, "stay in bed for a few days and get your strength back."

"I can't. That means they're winning. I will not give them the satisfaction of putting me out of action. I am having breakfast in the dining room at seven o'clock sharp."

Michael suffered discomfort all night. Aside from his body aching, his mind was in a turmoil. It was cold, but there was no wind blowing and the large building was dead quiet. Michael dozed for a short while but was awakened by the sound of wheels on the cobbles outside. The carriage was moving very slowly to limit the noise, but it was unsuccessful. This time, Michael wanted to see who was arriving. He was in the perfect place, Eliza's bedroom window looked over the courtyard, and he would've an ideal view.

Fighting the pain and dizziness, he struggled off the bed and shuffled to the window. He parted the drapes a sliver so that no one would see him. The carriage was plain and unmarked, unlike those of the aristocracy or clergy. It came to a halt at the side door. Michael's patience was rewarded when he witnessed Archbishop Donkin get out of the cab, followed by the limping Smithers.

Michael faced a dilemma. If he didn't act, some poor boy would be sodomised or worse, murdered, and It'd be on his conscience forever. He shuffled across the room and opened the door, barely able to stand, relying on the corridor wall to steady him. Michael was dressed in long johns and a vest, but he didn't care. He was dizzy from the bump on the head and the exhaustion that comes with struggling to breathe.

He hobbled, as far as the main staircase and then started to scream as loudly as his painful lungs would allow.

"Fire! Fire!" he bellowed.

He shouted it again and again until the doors opened and people began to evacuate the school, yelling and screaming as they ran down the hallways. Eventually the noise reached the attic and boys began pouring out of their dormitory then racing down the stairs. In the confusion, nobody saw Michael hiding in the gloom.

He made his way back to Eliza's room and peeped through the curtains. The courtyard was a chaotic jumble of adults and children yelling at each other in fear and relief. Secretly, all the boys wished that the evil place would burn to the ground and that the evil men inside It'd burn in hell.

The carriage stood waiting in the dark shadows of the school building. The crowd was distracted by the commotion and unaware of anything untoward. Michael didn't take his eyes off the coach for a second. He saw the narrow side door open. Donkin and Smithers emerged. In their black cassocks, they were almost invisible in the dead of night. They moved liked black ghosts until they reached the cab. As the pandemonium out on the assembly point on the road, only Michael saw the carriage leave the courtyard.

22

THE SECRET MEETING

Justine woke up when she heard her husband arrive home just before the larks would being to warble. She'd never paid attention to his comings and goings until Michael had raised her awareness with his curious questions.

She got out of bed and looked through the bedroom window. Paul was not alone. He'd Archbishop Donkin with him. A few minutes later another carriage arrived. Lord Sedgefield stepped out onto the driveway.

Justine put on her dressing gown and walked to the servant's staircase, barefoot. She made her way down the stairs avoiding all the creaky steps lest someone hear her. She tiptoed through the kitchen and into a service corridor. Without an oil lamp, she could barely see a thing. Tentatively, she made her way along holding onto the wall as a reference point, until her hand touched a door frame that led to the main hallway. Then slowly, she waved her hand beside her, silently hunting for the handle. Realising the door was already open, she ventured a few feet further then hid near the long curtains to plan her next move.

Three men were sitting in Paul's study, and fortunately for Justine, her husband had been reckless and left the door open. She tiptoed towards the light. The study was the only room in the house that had a light on. The old mansion had many ghostly nooks and crannies, and Justine hid in a dark alcove within hearing distance of the conversation.

She heard Paul offer his loathsome guests something to drink, and listened to the tinkle of ice in the crystal glasses while he poured. His friends waited silently. It'd be Donkin who finally spoke.

> "O'Neil has been taken care of once and for all," he said firmly. "Everything will be the same as before. We do not need to be concerned that our circle will be exposed by his meddling."
>
> "I agree," said Sedgefield, before adding with a chilling chuckle, "—unless he gets washed back up to the surface in his coffin and comes to haunt us."

The other two laughed contemptuously at the macabre joke.

> "Hayes cannot stand him, and he is convinced that O'Neil has something to do with Nel's disappearance. Besides, he was far too popular with the scholars. They trusted him."

"Peter has had his scuttlers search Salford, but nobody has seen Nel. I think the boy has run for it. He will not be back," Donkin said.

"What have you instructed Peter to do if he finds him?"

"That loose-tongued lad is a great risk to our operation," **Sedgefield** answered. "I have told Peter to dispose of him."

Out in the alcove, Justine was struggling to process what she was hearing. The conversation was surreal. She was becoming more distressed by what she was heard, but she could not move off the spot. She'd to listen to it all.

"Is Peter trustworthy?" asked Paul.

"Of course, he is. I pay him a lot of money to be loyal," said Sedgefield with a smirk.

Donkin laughed as Sedgefield explained further.

"Peter has helped Hayes solve the O'Neil problem. He returned to the school on Sunday night, and Hayes arranged a welcoming party for him by that rubbish heap next door to the school. We told Peter to finish the job."

Paul was as gleeful as a spoilt child at Christmas.

"Yes, well, that will make our lives much easier, jolly good show."

"I believe you knew the fellow in Ireland," quizzed Sedgefield. "You worked in similar parishes, did you not? You must have encountered each other frequently on your travels?"

Paul pulled a face.

"Well, I did not know that," murmured Donkin.

The truth was very close to the surface, and Paul was desperate to hide it by telling as much as he could risk, and manipulating the rest in his favour.

"Yes, we served the same parish in Ireland. He wasn't very popular with the Bishop of Dublin. They'd quite a few run-ins over the years. Seems he liked meddling and getting in the way there too."

"I believe he was dismissed," commented Sedgefield.

"Yes, he was. Terrible story—scandalous even."

"What happened?" Donkin asked, eager to hear how Michael had sinned.

"Adultery. He bedded somebody's wife, not that it was difficult, she was a brazen harlot so I heard," Paul said with distaste.

"Yes, yes, I understand. Word does get around, you know," said Lord Sedgefield with a knowing grin.

Paul felt uneasy—perhaps his marital secrets were not his own. Sedgefield laughed loudly.

"Now, Paul, you must admit that he is a very handsome man. Strapping and healthy. It's a pity that he is not inclined to the same pleasures we explore. I could have enjoyed him."

Paul struggled to keep his emotions intact. Everybody was close to, whether male or female, was attracted to Michael—except himself.

"There was a bit of gossip that you and O'Neil got into a little tussle at a festival? Is it true?" asked Donkin.

Paul's mouth opened and closed again.

"Is that why you did not greet each other at the school?" asked Sedgefield knowingly.

"Yes, yes," answered Paul, "He is a drunk. The day of the fight he'd had too many pints. I tried to help him, and—" Paul pointed to his knee, "—this was the outcome. He is a very dirty fighter. He picked up a rock and smashed my knee, crippled me for life."

"Well, I heard a different story," smirked Sedgefield.

"Dear God! No wonder you despise him," said Donkin, playing along.

"You may be lucky, Paul. If the scuttlers did a thorough job, we will find him dead atop the sewage tip tomorrow," laughed Sedgefield.

Paul hoped that the conversation would finally move on from scrutinising his nemesis. It was not to be.

"I noticed that he spoke to your wife for a very long time."

Paul blushed with embarrassment.

"Did they know each other in Bunratty?" asked Sedgefield.

"No, Justine lived on a farm. Her parents have a manor house in the country, and since she visited them frequently, she did not mix with the townsfolk much."

"That is strange" commented Donkin, "they'd an intense conversation in the hall."

Sedgefield chuckled.

"You heard what Paul told us, O'Neil is a womaniser."

"I note that your wife Justine is a lovely woman. I can appreciate her even if I do not desire her," commented the archbishop.

Sedgefield helped himself to another large measure of scotch.

"I heard that O'Neil could charm any Irish woman into bed, even most pious wives in the community."

"Yes. I believe the Archbishop of Dublin was furious," muttered Paul.

"Well, at least he did not try and seduce your wife, Smithers," said Sedgefield sarcastically.

"Agreed," said a relieved Paul. "Justine is so innocent and naïve, always been, since the day we met."

"It took her weeks to consummate our marriage," lied Paul. "Poor little thing, she was terrified. But which man can tolerate frigidity from his wife? The frustration was too much for me, and I was forced to find other sources of pleasure."

"Yes," said Donkin. "I can understand that."

"If my dalliances ever became known. I am sure that the church would secretly support me in this matter."

"Of course," said Sedgefield.

"Woman are made to have children and that is all. The ancient Greeks understood it perfectly. I have never found a woman that can please me as much as a boy can," said Smithers.

Sedgefield nodded in agreement.

"I must say I do prefer the boys. Six years old is probably the correct age. The older ones fight back. Little Jono was my favourite. It was a pity that he screamed so much. Thank God, Peter was there to solve the problem," lamented Donkin.

"Yes, how did Peter eventually dispose of the body?" asked Sedgefield.

"Oh, he shoved him under a flagstone between two graves. Peter said that if there is ever a search for him, and we need to move the body, the name to look for is Edwards and Edwards. A husband and wife buried beside each other," replied Donkin.

"Such a pity. I had high hopes for Jono," said Paul, shaking his head.

"Enough of this grim talk, gentlemen. We have a fresh intake of boys in two weeks, and we will be ready for them."

23

JUSTINE THE WARRIOR

After hearing the awful conversation unfold and the men sink further into slurred drunken banter, Justine instantly transformed into a lioness protecting her cubs. She crept past the open door and ran back upstairs as quietly as she could and knocked quietly on Mrs Diggery's door.

"What is wrong?" asked Mrs Diggery, "has something happened."

"The children must sleep in my room from now on. I do not want them alone in the nursery at night, and if I go out, they must sleep in your room," ordered Justine.

"Yes, of course," Mrs Diggery agreed. "Are they in danger?"

"Yes, I believe so," replied Justine.

"But who would want to hurt them? Surely not one of the staff. We always check their references are exemplary," Mrs Diggery asked frantic with worry.

"Their father, or any of his friends that visit this house. I have discovered something terrible."

"Oh, no!" exclaimed the nursemaid.

"In the longer term, I need to get them away from here," said Justine. "Although, I must confess I am currently at a loss as to how I will achieve that."

Mrs Diggery nodded in support of the protective decision.

"I'll do anything I can to help. You can rely on me."

Justine heard footsteps coming up the stairs. She and Mrs Diggery rushed to the nursery. Neither of them would allow Smithers to be alone with Rosie and Hope.

Justine, for years relegated to the role of the submissive wife, had returned to her old self. The endless humiliation rose to the surface, and galvanised her into the furious Celtic warrior she was born to be.

"Mrs Diggery, I need you to go to Corning Street school. It's in Angel Meadow, so be careful. I don't need to remind you how dangerous it is. Replace my old friend from Ireland Michael O'Neil. I don't know what Paul and his friends have done to him, but I need to know if he is alive and not dead in the waste ground next to it."

"Heavens! He can't be dead! What sort of monsters are these men?" said the anxious old woman.

"I need you to be strong," Justine whispered firmly. "This matter affects every boy in that school. If Michael is not already dead, he is in terrible danger."

"Don't worry, lass. I will do exactly as you ask," she promised Justine.

"If he is capable, tell him to meet me at St. Mary's Church, Mulberry Street, Manchester tomorrow at five o'clock. Tell him that I know what is happening at the school, and I will help him."

Mrs Diggery nodded.

"Of course, my dear. I will find him. You can count on me."

"Don't tell anybody that I sent you. Think up a story. Tell them you are looking for laundry work. Anything. Just get to him."

*

Eliza brought Michael his clean clothes. His body was stiff from the beating, and every muscle fought his decision to flex it. Desperate to stay where he was, he'd to conjure up the will to move. Eliza made him tea heaped with sugar, and after he drank it, he felt a little better.

After he lumbered his way up to sit on the edge of the bed, she washed his face gently, wiping off all the last of the dried blood, then helped him into his day clothes. She buttoned his shirt and then sat on her knees in front of him, helping ease his trousers over his bruised outstretched legs.

Michael looked down at her. There was no doubt he'd become fond of her over time. In the moments that he was lonely and desolate, he'd thought of seeking comfort from her. If he'd no conscience, he would've married her. They could have had a good life together but Michael pushed those thoughts aside. He could not commit to another woman before he knew that there was no possibility of ever being with Justine.

He didn't understand what kept him holding onto the dream, despite it seeming doomed. She was married to a powerful man, and he knew divorce was not a realistic option.

He could not hurt Eliza. She didn't deserve it, and so he remained satisfied to keep things platonic. The best he could hope for was that she would one day meet a man who was as tender as she was.

"Thank you, Eliza," he whispered.

"What are friends for?" she smiled and touched his face gently.

It was more painful going down the stairs than up. He felt every muscle in his body creak with reluctance. He was exhausted and shaking when he reached the bottom. Before he entered the dining hall, he stood up the best he could. Like a music hall entertainer about to perform in front of the crowd, it was showtime.

Michael's boys were shocked to see their master so severely beaten. Even by The Meadow standards, he was in a bad way. Some of the older lads jumped up from their benches and rushed forward to help him.

> "Sit down at once," screeched Hayes like a banshee, but they ignored him and went to their teacher's aide.
>
> "Sit down now, I command you," continued Hayes. "You'll receive six of the best from the birch if you do not obey me."
>
> "Oh up, yer arse," one of the boys shouted at Hayes coupled with an ugly hand gesture.

They walked him to the seats where the Hayes and the teachers dined. Michael passed Peter and the gang, who were at their usual table and their smug presence dominated the room. He found great pleasure in watching their faces as he passed by, even in his battered state. It was apparent that they believed they'd left him for dead. Yet, here he was, resurrected—black and blue, yes—but alive.

Kevin pulled out a chair for Michael and the older boys lowered him into it. Michael felt proud of his pupils.

They'd risked the wrath of the scuttlers to help him, and he would never forget it.

By now, the teachers and support staff were crowding around him, asking question. Aside from feeling claustrophobic, he also felt nauseous with anxiety.

"Give him space, chaps," begged young Mr Conrad, "he needs some air."

Hayes gave a condescending look from the head of the table.

"What happened to you? What sort of example are you sending to the boys?"

"Leave him alone," ordered Grant Conrad fiercely.

"No, it's fine Grant. It's an excellent question. So, Mr Hayes, what did happen? Would you care to enlighten me?"

Hayes pushed his breakfast round on his plate and said nothing. Michael was in no condition to push the matter. He didn't have the energy for it.

Mr Burbidge walked into the dining room as he did every other school day. He'd prepared to make the daily announcements, and his eyes scoured the tables to see which teachers were in attendance. It took a few seconds to register that the strange man sitting in Michael's seat—was Michael.

"Mr Hayes, what happened to O'Neil?" demanded Burbidge in a loud voice.

When there was no response, the headmaster strode over to his deputy.

"I asked you a question, Mr Hayes! What has happened to Mr O'Neil?"

"I have no idea, sir," said Hayes, putting up his hands and feigning ignorance.

"That is not an acceptable answer, Hayes."

He turned around and faced the hall.

"Boys, who will tell me what has happened to Mr O'Neil?" Burbidge asked in a harsh voice.

A hand went up at one of the tables.

"Yes. You—Finlay, stand up."

Michael was close to fainting.

"Mr O'Neil was severely beaten last night, Mr Burbidge. He could hardly breathe, and he could not walk. It happened on the waste land next door. Judging by the state of his clothes, they left him lying on all that filth—left him for dead, Sir."

Peter looked at Hayes anxiously. They would've to silence Kevin Finlay before he became more of a nuisance.

"Where did you get those details, Finlay? Leaving the dormitory is a punishable offence. You'll be thrashed until your arse bleeds," shouted Hayes.

Burbidge looked at the hostel master in shock.

"Tell me!" shouted Hayes. "Which one of you little wretches found him, and I will take care of you."

"Be quiet, Mr Hayes. This is no time for your theatrics. Calm down."

Hayes had never believed that Mr Burbidge had a backbone, so he was shocked to be experiencing his wrath for the first time.

Michael heard a lot of whispering and shuffling, and then he saw all of the boys in the dining room take to their feet, each lad's chair legs dragging noisily along the wooden floor.

"I found him," shouted a voice.

"No, I found him," shouted another.

"You're lying, I did!" shouted someone from the back.

A wee lad jumped up on the table.

"No, sir, it was me!" he cried.

Hayes was dumbfounded. He'd never witnessed such an act of defiance before. Michael's boys were fearless. One by one, they claimed responsibility for finding their master.

Burbidge looked at his assistant with disgust.

> "Well, that settles that, Mr Hayes. These young men behaved like I would expect them to. One of them acted responsibly and saved Mr O'Neil from certain death, and they all saved the boy responsible from your cruel vindictiveness. Well done, young men, I am very proud of you today."

Michael collapsed on the table and lost consciousness. The last thing he heard was Burbidge telling Hayes to shut up.

24

LIFE AND DEATH

Mrs Diggery arrived at the school around mid-morning, long after the furore in the dining room was over. When she asked to see Mr O'Neil, the old secretary looked at her uncomfortably, not sure how much information he could share with her.

"Madam, he is very ill at this time and unable to see visitors."

"Ill?" asked Mrs Diggery.

"What is your business with Mr O'Neil?" the secretary demanded.

Mrs Diggery was quick on her feet.

"I am his aunt," she replied.

Endless questions and tittle-tattle that day had seen the secretary falling behind with his tasks for the day. Keen to make some progress, the secretary weakened.

"—I suppose I can tell you."

"Is something wrong with him?"

"Yes, he was involved in an accident last night. He is seriously ill. Injuries to his head and abdomen mainly."

"Where is he now?" Mrs Diggery asked firmly.

"He is in his room. We are taking care of him."

"I want to see him immediately,"

"Of course. It's fortunate that you have arrived. You'll be able to care for him better than we can. We have lots of new boys arriving and we need to prepare."

"Head wounds sound serious," said Mrs Diggery. "Replace somebody to show me to his room immediately. The sooner we can get him back to the family house the better."

The secretary disappeared for a short while and came back with a young Irish woman.

"This is Eliza, and she will help you."

Eliza waited until she was out of earshot of the secretary.

"Don't be shocked when you see him—he is in a terrible state."

"Dear God above, what happened to him?"

"He was beaten to within an inch of his life by some thugs that roam the streets," she answered.

"Who did it to him?" asked Mrs Diggery.

"I have my suspicions, but I will keep it to myself for now. Talk is dangerous," answered Eliza.

"I understand."

"Are you his aunt?" asked Eliza.

"No."

"Then who are you? I cannot allow strangers near him," demanded Eliza.

"Let me put it this way. I represent somebody who loves him very much. A concerned parishioner he knew in Ireland."

Eliza opened the door to Michael's room. Mrs Diggery stepped in and walked over to the bed and looked down at the patient. His face was a mess. His head was severely swollen where he'd received the cruel blows, and both of his eyes were beaten closed. She looked at him enraged. Besides this being the love of Justine Smithers life, this was her fellow countryman, and how dare somebody do this to him.

"He has broken ribs, and it's a wonder that he hasn't fractured his skull. His body is full of puncture wounds where they kicked him with those horrid clogs some of the scuttler lads wear about these streets."

Mrs Diggery could see what Eliza meant. The young woman worried she'd said too much. She didn't want to be at the wrong end of the gang's fury.

"Michael needs better care than this. He needs a full-time nurse if those wounds are not to go septic. Sometimes he knows where he is, and at other times he doesn't."

Mrs Diggery sat down on the edge of the bed, her face flooded with compassion for the broken man. Eliza gave them a brief moment alone.

"Hello, Michael," she smiled.

"That is a Kildare accent I hear there," he mumbled.

"I am Mrs Diggery."

"Ah, you sent me the letter."

"Yes, I did. Do you know anybody that I can contact to help you? You need proper nursing care."

"Father McDermott, Liverpool," he whispered.

"Right."

"Tell Justine to be careful. I think you might know why?"

"You can rely on me, Mr O'Neil."

*

Hayes stood in Archbishop Donkin's ornate office, pacing in front of the desk. Sedgefield sat reading the paper.

"You and your friends need to lay off the lads. Stay away from the school for a while, eh? Things are getting tricky."

"We make a good income out of this little business," said Donkin, irritated. "Some of our patrons are prepared to pay up to a thousand pounds for a few evenings of live entertainment. Given they'll want to keep the secret as much as we do, I am sure things will be fine. We can always pay off—or bump off—a few meddling bobbies."

"Burbidge is furious with me. I am sure he will want to sack me."

"Your job is safe, Hayes," said Sedgefield, "You're far too valuable to us. We'll never allow Burbidge to dismiss you."

"That is by-the-by. Everybody needs to lie low and let the dust settle. I have sent Peter off on a little holiday to London for a while. Everybody knows that he was the one who almost killed O'Neil. What else are the plods going to uncover if they come sniffing round?"

"Perhaps you're right," said Donkin. "We are putting the whole operation in jeopardy for a little short-term gain. We'll need a few months for this whole episode to blow over. It would've been much easier if he died as we intended."

"If he dies at the school, there will surely be an inquest. All you need is a child like Nel to mouth off about what has been happening when the coroner comes to visit, and—well—we'll have a much bigger problem than stalling profits," Hayes warned.

"This is unfortunate. We have people on waiting lists. Hayes," whined Sedgefield.

"You don't understand the mood in the hostel. I was anticipating an uprising. Your impatience could put us out of business."

The archbishop listened carefully before Sedgefield snapped and gave his edict on how to deal with the problems.

"With Michael O'Neil out of the picture, you should've enough time to get them under control. We'll resume business next week. We cannot afford to stop for months. I will not hear of it," **Sedgefield** said fiercely.

*

Mrs Diggery returned to the Smithers' house well into the afternoon. She found Justine waiting anxiously in the garden.

"What **happened?" asked** the lady of the house.

"He is in a frightful state, lass. I will be honest with you. He looks far worse than I expected."

"I am going to fetch him," said Justine determinedly, "I will hide him in this house if I must, or take him to a hospital."

"He is more likely to die in a hospital than at the school," answered Mrs Diggery. "Them places are full of disease. Besides that's not what he wants."

"Don't tell me he is being stubborn again! Is there someone looking after him there?"

"Yes, a young Irish girl called Eliza."

"Could he speak to you?"

"Yes, he told me to find a 'Father McDermott' in Liverpool. Michael said that McDermott would know what to do."

"So, it seems clear. One of us, must go to Liverpool and find this McDermott fellow and ask for his help. I think it'll be easier for you to go. I cannot let the children out of my sight, and even if they accompanied me, Paul would be more determined looking for me than you. I will tell everybody that I have given you a few days off. My husband won't suspect anything for a while at least. You can be in Liverpool in less than two hours."

Justine lay in her bed and listened to the storm raging outside. The rain was beating against the panes. Any harder, and she was sure It'd break the glass. She got up to check that the windows were closed tightly and saw water was running down the street like a river.

She closed the curtains and tested the door to make sure that it was locked. *Yes.* She was exhausted, and climbed into her warm bed, a child on either side of her. The attack had made Justine rethink her priorities. She wished that Michael could be with them, then It'd be perfect. Somehow, there had to be a way to be together. *We wouldn't be the first star-crossed lovers to run away to a new start.*

25

A BROTHER'S LOVE

Water flooded through the cemetery at St. Michael's flags in Angel Meadow. Black clouds spewed rain and sleet, and it transformed the ground into a muddy and slushy expanse. Forty thousand corpses lay beneath the soil, piled one upon the other in mass graves. As the water soaked into the earth around the dead, the pressure pushed the coffins up. The water raised the flagstones until the hill, allocated as a peaceful and final resting place, was transformed into a writhing mound of death.

Miraculously Mr and Mrs Edwards remained under the flagstones, but little Jono was unearthed as the rain washed away the shallow soil surrounding him. The youngster was just another corpse in a pile of many. Nobody knew who he was, and nobody cared to find out. Water flushed over him, gathering the residue from his decomposing body, and washing it out of the cemetery. The foetid water formed filthy rivulets which joined to form a stream of detritus which coursed through the Meadow's streets and into the filthy River Irk.

The gravediggers had the grisly duty of reinterring the corpses. When they found what was left of Jono, they were too lazy to seek a coffin, so they shoved him back into the wet earth between Edwards and Edwards, thumping the soil down with their spades in an attempt to keep him there.

Two days after the flood, a carriage arrived at the school doors. Two Jesuit priests emerged and asked to see Mr O'Neil. They made their way up the rickety back stairs and found his room. The man lying on the bed was close to death. It mattered not. He was a brother, and they'd come to fetch him and ensured he convalesced. The woman tending him was doing the best she could to keep him alive. The strange men showed Eliza a note from Mrs Diggery and that the priests were there to assist.

She helped them carry Michael's pain-wracked, fever-riddled body to the carriage. They lay him on the seat as gently as they could. They vowed protect him, and they prayed to the Virgin that he would survive.

The two Jesuits delivered Michael to a convent in Liverpool. It stood a long way back from the old coaching route, in a beautiful, safe, and peaceful garden.

The nuns washed him and tended his wounds. They applied special tinctures and administered ancient herbal medicines to break his fever. They lay him in a warm, clean bed and summoned Father McDermott in case he was needed to console the man in his last hours.

McDermott arrived at the convent within the hour. He seemed troubled man and his lively personality was unusually sombre. He'd only recently met Michael, but from what he could gauge, he was a good man who didn't deserve such a brutal beating.

Father McDermott sat on a chair next to Michael's bed and watched him sleeping. Occasionally, Michael would stir, and mumble in his delirium. Father McDermott was reluctant to administer Michael's last rights. It'd symbolise that he'd given up, and he didn't want this man to die. Besides, he wasn't a Catholic and Michael hadn't been excommunicated.

Father McDermott was still sombre when he saw Mother Superior.

> "This man is going to survive," said McDermott. "This man is not going to die. He still has work to do here on earth."
>
> "I doubt we can give him the will to live, Father. His spirit seems as broken as his body. He cuts a lonely figure."
>
> "Don't worry about that, Mother. I will send for a person I know that can revive him better than any tincture."

Mrs Diggery received a letter from Father McDermott, delivered by a special envoy dressed in civilian clothing.

The letter stated that Michael O'Neil required particularly tender care, and it was his opinion that Justine was the only person who could give him the strength to live.

Justine approached her husband in his study. Paul was spending more evenings at home, and it was evident that no one was feeding his depraved sexual appetite, because he'd come to her bedroom door twice and ordered her to open it.

He was beginning to realise his submissive little wife really was gone, never to return. She was livid when it came to her husband. Justine would never allow him near her again. For her, it was only a matter of time before she would testify against him and his depraved cabal. It'd soon be their turn to taste a complete loss of freedom. The thought gave her a glimmer of hope. *They'll be in jail for the rest of their lives.* He tried the door several times, but she ignored it, grateful that her two children were lying in her arms, safe from their father. The furniture she'd stacked up against the only entrance, night after night, added to that sense of security.

"I have received a letter from Ireland. My mother is gravely ill, and she has insisted that she see the children before she dies," Justine lied.

Paul looked at her thoughtfully, not really caring if she was telling the truth or lying. Either way, her forthcoming absence was good news. With Justine away, he could fully utilise the mansion. There was plenty of space in the cellars. Peter had been tasked with finding some fresh meat for them in London, and, providing they were discrete, the boys could be brought back to his house. He knew that Donkin and Sedgefield would be delighted operations could resume, albeit only for a short time, should things remain too difficult at the school. He decided to exclude the Hayes. He could no longer be trusted to keep things ticking over smoothly. The man was a menace.

"I will be leaving in the morning, and Mrs Diggery will be accompanying me to look after the children."

"How long will you be away?" he asked her without looking up from the documents he was reading.

"A minimum of six weeks. As you know, it's a fair way to travel."

Justine was expecting him to explode but for once in their married life, Paul Smithers was remarkably accommodating. It puzzled her, worried her, but she couldn't let that stop her plans.

"I suggest that you take all the time you need. The family are very important, and the children will love farm life."

Justine Smithers could not pack her bags quick enough.

*

When Father McDermott opened the door, he took one look at the wild beauty that was Justine and knew exactly why Michael had fallen in love with her.

"I trust you'll all stay here?"

Father McDermott was so firm, yet welcoming, that Justine did not even consider arguing.

He introduced the young family to Nel and Mrs Bunting, who was delighted to see another two children that she could add to her instant family. The housekeeper took the youngsters off to the kitchen promising them a hot cocoa.

"Let us go to the drawing room," father McDermott said to Justine. "I imagine that you have a lot of questions for me."

Exhausted, she followed him and sat down on a plush leather chair in front of the glowing fireplace.

"After the day that you have had, I expect that a stiff drink will be in order rather than cocoa? I hope you drink!" he said, raising his eyebrows mischievously.

"Of course, I do," Justine answered, catching on to his humour.

Once the drinks were poured, the upbeat mood in the room darkened. There was no escaping reality.

"Michael is not doing well," confessed Father McDermott.

Justine's eyes filled with tears.

"Now, Justine, we cannot afford to lose hope if we want him to live. You're my secret weapon in the fight for his wellbeing."

"And I assure you, I will not fail you—or him. Let us make a start. Take me to the convent. I will stay there until he is fully recovered. I will care for him night and day. May the consequences be damned—I will never leave him again."

Father McDermott smiled at Justine. For the second time that evening, he understood why Michael, the firebrand former priest, had fallen in love with the feisty female before him.

"Well, then, we'd better get you over there—but finish your drink first, perhaps? You'll need it. It's going to be a long night."

*

Justine spoke to Mrs Diggery.

"Father McDermott will escort you and the children to the harbour tomorrow morning. He will put you on the ferry to Ireland and give you a letter for the Archbishop of Dublin who will arrange transport to my parent's farm. You'll be safe there. Except for my parents, do not tell anyone in Bunratty that I stayed behind in Liverpool. I must help Michael. He cannot face this alone. After all, I am the reason that he is teaching in Angel Meadow. Who knows what these men will do if they find where he is?"

26

ENOUGH LIFE FOR BOTH OF THEM

Justine stood next to the bed and looked down at Michael. His arms were severely cut and bruised where the sharp clogs had dug into him. His scalp was still swollen around the wound to the back of his head. *How bad he must have looked on the night he crawled back to the school?* She lifted the sheet at the side and saw the deep lacerations on his legs and his stomach. His chest was tightly bandaged. He wreaked of carbolic soap. It was clear, the nuns and nurses had done the best that they could under the circumstances.

"We do not know what more to do for him," said the desperate Mother Superior to Justine, as they watched the nurse at work.

The woman took his pulse and felt his forehead temperature with the back of her hand. She looked over to a young nun in the corner.

"Sister, send somebody to find a chemist that supplies carbolic acid, we'll need more. And ask if they have lead-infused tincture. And opium, we'll need that to manage the pain once he fully regains consciousness."

The poor nun didn't know what the nurse planned to do, nor what the concoctions would do, but did what she was asked.

It was time for Justine to provide succour. She took a chair and sat by his bedside. Michael heard her talking to him. Her voice was soft. She held his hand and stroked a lone patch of unbroken skin on his forearm.

"Michael, my love. It's me, Justine. I am with you."

If it was a dream, Michael didn't want it to end. She leant towards his ear.

"Michael, you have to listen to me. I am here to look after you. Please open your eyes for me."

Her mouth was so close he could feel her gentle breathing and hear her loving words motivating him to respond. His eyelids flickered, but he was struggling to fight through the haze that enveloped his mind.

"Justine," he murmured.

"Yes, I am here. You're going to live, Michael, and you, me, and the girls—we are going to be together forever. I promise."

A tear ran down Michael's cheek. He couldn't open his eyes, move his body, or speak, but he knew that he could trust her word, and that she was worth the fight. The lone tear told Justine he was listening, and it bolstered her confidence that McDermott's plan would work.

It was time to change his dressings and Justine was invited to unwrap Michael's bandages. He groaned in pain. His chest was a mass of bruises joining together in a big purple mess. Thankfully, Eliza had strapped him tightly which had helped keep his ribs in place. The nurse made a mixture of lead tincture and opium and drenched the bandages in it. Then she strapped him up again. Inspecting his body from head-to-toe, she decided that the source of his problems was the terribly infected wound on his head. It was still swollen and had turned septic **overnight**, oozing endless yellow pus into the pillow.

She instructed the nuns to melt bars of soap and mix it with the carbolic acid.

> "Nobody is to come near him without washing their hands with that soap. When wash him, we will use it as then too," she instructed them.

Instead, of taking offence, the nuns showed great interest in this modern form of medicine that Justine was demonstrating. Ancient herbal remedies were one thing, but some of the new treatments made modern day miracles a daily occurrence.

"I am going to clean this head wound. It's severely infected. He must not lie on it. He must have his head to one side all the time, even if you have to tie him down. We'll not put a bandage on it anymore, and we need to get it dry."

The nuns were confused. In their world, all wounds needed to be covered and protected from the miasma. What was this woman telling them? They looked puzzled.

"Trust me, ladies. The wound must stay uncovered, and it needs to air. We'll clean it three times a day with carbolic acid."

The nuns gave Justine a bowl of hot water and the carbolic soap that the nurse had ordered. She used a razor and as gently as possible she began to shave the hair around the wound. Slowly, Justine began to clean the area with water. As soon as she was satisfied that she'd done her best, she began to disinfect the wound itself with diluted carbolic acid and insisted that they remove everything that Michael was wearing, noticing some of the other wounds were on the turn too.

"You cannot!" exclaimed the shocked Mother Superior.

"I will," replied the determined Justine. "This is a life-and-death matter, a time for modern medicine, not a time to be restricted by the bible."

One thing that was done religiously was Justine dribbling small amounts of water into Michael's parched mouth. She slept in a chair next to his bed for three days, and on the fourth day, he woke up.

Michael looked up at the massive domed ceiling, then around the room, slowly taking in his surroundings. He touched the wound at the back of his head, and there was no blood on his fingers. Michael felt weak and nauseous. He moved his head slowly and saw Justine asleep next to his bed. Justine's wild dark hair was fanned around her face. Looking so peaceful he didn't want to wake her. He lay and watched her for a while. Then the temptation was too great, he'd to speak to her.

"Justine," he called quietly, "Justine, where are the girls?"

Justine's eyes flew open, and she smiled. Her eyes sparkled, and then she put back her head and laughed loudly. Then, she cried from relief. Michael was going to live.

Justine sat on the side of the bed and took his hand.

"How long have I been here?"

"Nearly a week," she explained with a loving smile. "The children and Mrs Diggery are with my parents in Ireland, and they're safe."

Michael smiled back at her, feeling his dry lips crack with the movement.

"You need to eat. We need to get your strength up," announced Justine.

"You sound like Sister Julia," he chuckled, "and I feel like I am six years old again."

She fed him soup and some bread, instead of being sick, he was ravishingly hungry and asked for more. His body was still stiff, and his ribs ached from time to time, but he felt in far better shape than when he arrived.

It was late afternoon, and the room was filled with the warm hues that are only visible when the sun rises and sets. Soft golden light flooded the room. With the nuns at silent prayer, there was no noise except for the songbirds rustling in the trees preparing to roost for the night.

"Come here," said Michael and lifted the bed covers invitingly. "We get another night alone."

"This is a convent, Michael," whispered Justine.

"Lock the door."

Justine went over to the door and turned the hefty iron key and walked back to his bed.

"Now, take off your clothes," he whispered.

Justine undressed in front of him, without feeling shy or shame. Michael opened the bed covers, and she slid in next to him. He felt her body against him and absorbed her energy. He knew that it was her energy that had willed him to live, and he loved her for it. He wanted to feel her lying next to him, so he could absorb much more. He kissed forehead and repeatedly told her that he loved her, and she lay in his arms enjoying feeling him close to once more. They fell asleep together and slept as soundly as children. Justine refused to let him go and held onto him all night.

In the morning, their thoughts turned to the future.

"I have to go back to the school, Justine. Those men—"

"I know. We'll go back together."

"What?"

"We'll go back together, Michael," she repeated slowly.

Michael looked puzzled and wondered if his tongue had wagged in his delirious state.

"But it's my problem. I am their teacher," he argued, not wanting to put her in any danger.

"I overheard my husband talking to Donkin and Sedgefield on the night of your attack. I know what is happening there, and we must stop it. Those poor boys are counting on us."

27

FACING THE BEASTS

Justine and Michael reached Manchester long after dark. He'd insisted that they return as soon as possible. His wounds weren't sufficiently healed, but Justine agreed that it was critical to prevent the abuse of the children going any further. Unable to tell the nuns the true reason for their sudden departure, the ladies thought the pair mad for upping sticks so soon after the assault.

Justine had never been through Angel Meadow, and the scene that met her was one of abominable poverty, living conditions that she'd not imagined possible.

The streets and alleys were congested, even-though it was the middle of the night. With the latest technical advances in lighting, the factories were able to work non-stop producing goods that would be shipped around the globe, making the mightiest empire in the world mightier yet.

It was the population density that struck her the most. She'd never seen so many people in such a small place. She observed the drunkards, pimps and prostitutes that littered the dark alleyways. She studied the ragged little children on their way to and from their night shifts. Justine realised how easy it was to coax rural folk to move to the industrial heartlands with the promise of better lodgings, better opportunities, round bellies full of food and happy heads filled with education. They were easy to exploit because even the slightest comfort sounded like a blessing to them, and they stayed even when it wasn't provided.

"Are you feeling upset?" asked Michael.

"No," she replied, "I feel grateful that I don't have to live this way."

They walked the winding streets until Justine saw a church.

"Ironically, that church is called St. Michaels," he told her.

"It looks as hopeless as the rest," said Justine.

"Yes, the locals aren't very impressed by it. They say it's the ugliest church that they have ever seen."

Justine could make out a few headstones, but not many.

"Is this a cemetery?" she asked him.

"Yes, it is. The cemetery is called St. Michael's Flags."

Justine didn't answer. Her wheels were turning, trying to work out the significance of the name. As they walked in silence, things came back to her.

"So, this is where they dumped little Jono," Justine gasped. "His body is somewhere on this macabre hill."

"It's a massive area. There are thousands of bodies up there. Without more details, we'll never be able to give the lad a proper burial."

Justine looked heartbroken.

"I hate those men for that they did to him."

She thought back to the overheard conversation, hoping it might trigger something useful to be recalled.

"I'm missing something. I know I am."

The couple wandered through the graveyard, trying to read the chiselled names in the gloom.

"That's it!" said Justine, pointing dramatically at one of the stones. "Edwards and Edwards. Edward is my father's middle name. It made me think of him when they said the words."

*

"Donkin and his friends are arriving tonight," Hayes said to Peter. "I trust you will make sure that everything runs smoothly. Word of this must not leak out to any of the boys, and we do not need hysterics, or nosey parkers. What with Nel being missing and O'Neil on the loose somewhere, we need to be vigilant. Walls have ears."

Peter nodded. He'd a newfound confidence after the all-expenses paid trip to London and the new profit-sharing arrangement with the syndicate. In his damaged gangland mind, he'd suddenly realised his worth and was being paid for it. He was no longer a common Scuttler, he was one of the leaders of a highly profitable criminal enterprise, and now he could command respect. He'd become an underworld boss overnight, and the power was dazzling.

"I will handpick the stock tonight," said Hayes, gleefully.

Hayes lit a lamp, and the two men prepared to open the door to the dormitory. Inside, each bed held a little lad, and it was up to Hayes to choose whom he would expose to the wealthy men wanting a good night of carnal entertainment. Sometimes they were chosen for their looks, sometimes to make them more compliant in lessons.

"Kevin Finlay is proving to be a menace," whispered Hayes. "He is far too close to O'Neil. Let's teach him a lesson for starters."

Peter opened his pocket notebook and jotted down the name, deep in thought.

> "It's a pity that Nel disappeared when he did," said boy. "I would like to have seen him squirm a little."

> "There was that wee one who jumped on the table and cheered for O'Neil. Where is he?" asked Hayes. "They'll learn that if they cross us, they'll pay. Oh yes, and there was that little scoundrel who dared to show me the finger. We'll take him as well. How **many's** that?"

> "Three, Mr Hayes. We need another two. Donkin said that there would be two extra men with them tonight. Let's pick those two boys based on their physique then. The first ones aren't exactly 'lookers'."

Peter prepared to dispatch his team of scuttlers with military precision, keen to avoid another mess.

> "Right, you two. This lists the five boys we have chosen for the night. Get them down to the cellar, pronto. Our guests will arrive at any time soon."

Peter watched his boys creep toward the beds quietly. The young boys were fast asleep, secure in the knowledge that nobody had accosted them since Michael had left. Without making a sound, the scuttlers covered their boys' mouths. The children woke up feeling themselves being picked up by rough hands. They only realised what was happening when they reached the door, and by then it was too late.

Kevin Finlay fought his oppressors down the stairs, until Peter gave him a hard crack over the head to quieten him. He misjudged the force required. Dazed, the poor boy's legs buckled underneath him, and he fell to the ground. Peter kicked him in the ribs to remind him to stand, but he didn't. The hosts shut the door and set about the final preparations for the sordid soiree.

The boys looked around the cellar with large eyes. The area was comfortably furnished and looked like a study. There were plenty of comfortable chairs scattered around the room, and bottles of alcohol were neatly stacked on a table, ready for a party. Kevin Finlay began to come around, and immediately began to scream as loudly as he could, in the vain hope that somebody would hear him, but nobody could hear a sound, the walls were solid stone.

*

Justine and Michael sneaked up to his old room, darting from one patch of darkness to the next. Michael knew the routine for the visitors all too well. It was time for the waiting game to begin. He trained his ear to listen out for the tell-tale rumble of carriage wheels. He lay on his old bed, fully clothed and Justine lay under the blanket next to him. He watched her resting and stroked her hair, knowing that he could never leave her again. He thought about the two little angels who were so like their mother and wondered if he would make a good father to them. Running away to a far-flung place where no-one knew them seemed a glorious prospect.

He knew that the trio would arrive soon. Sundays after work were one of Donkin's favourite times to visit. Michael second-guessed he liked to unwind after a hard day of keeping his mask of respectability on as he preached to his congregation.

The rain almost drowned out the sound of the wheels rolling slowly over the cobbles, but Michael was alert. He sat up and shook Justine gently.

"I think one of them has arrived," he said.

Michael hobbled down to Eliza's bedroom and knocked on her door, quietly, but with urgency. She opened up and stood dumbfounded for a few seconds, wondering if it was Michael or his ghost before her.

"Michael!" she said and put out her hand to touch him.

It wasn't Eliza he'd come to see, though, it was the vista. He pushed straight past and went to the window. He parted the curtains slightly and peered down into the courtyard.

Two coaches had stopped outside the side door, and he was anxious to see who was inside. Eventually, the side entrance of the school was opened, and Michael watched Hayes standing in the doorway, beckoning for the men to come in.

From up above, he watched three men get out of the first coach—Donkin, Sedgefield and the limping Smithers bringing up the rear. The other two in the second coach were foreign to him.

"Eliza, do you know where Mr Burbidge lives?" asked Michael. "I want you to fetch him and bring the police."

"What is happening, Michael? Will you please explain yourself?"

"Eliza, the lads, are in danger from Donkin and his cronies. I'll explain more later. You need to fetch Burbidge. Be careful. Leave through the front door. It's the most direct route. If Peter catches you, he will kill you to protect himself."

Eliza put on her clothes hurriedly, covered her head in a dark shawl and slipped down the stairs as quietly as she could. She opened the front door to the freezing gale, and ran to the headmaster's house as fast as she could. She frantically knocked on the door, creating enough noise to wake up the street, but there was no reply. She struck again, slamming her knuckles against the wood so hard that they started to bleed.

Mr Burbidge eventually answered the door in his dressing-gown, his wife, stood behind him.

"What on earth, Eliza," he exclaimed. "What are you doing here at this time?"

"Mr O'Neil says you must come immediately," said Eliza. "Something terrible is happening at the school, and you need to be there."

"O'Neil? I had given him up for dead."

"No, sir, he is very much alive. He has Bishop Smithers' wife with him, come quickly, sir, this is urgent."

"Is it a fire? Have those bloody stairs collapsed? I told Hayes to get a carpenter to look at them," whittered Mr Burbidge flustered.

"No, Sir. I can't speak about it here on the doorstep. Mr O'Neil will tell you everything. Please come now."

She tugged at his arm. He pulled away angrily.

"Please, headmaster. Now! Michael says to bring the police with us. We can find a bobby on his beat."

"God Almighty! What the hell has he done now?"

"It has something to do with Donkin and the boys in the cellar. The pupils are in grave danger. Why else would Michael put himself in such danger to return to help them if the threat wasn't real? Someone wants Mr O'Neil dead!"

A few of the boys awoke as Michael manoeuvred himself through the attic looking for Kevin Finlay.

"Where does he sleep?" Michael asked a small boy.

"There, sir, there, next to the window."

Michael rushed over, but the bed was empty. He felt a sense of despair. As his eyes adjusted to the darkness, he counted there were number of empty beds. There were five in total. He owed Kevin Finlay a debt of gratitude for saving him when he was severely beaten. Kevin could easily have run away and reported the unfortunate event to Hayes, who would've finished Michael off with a smile. Instead, the boy had been loyal and steadfast If it were not for Kevin and Eliza, Michael would be dead.

By now, all the boys in the attic were awake.

> "You need to be quiet as mice," warned Michael, "your friends in the cellar are in grave danger. I need to fetch them now. I can't protect you and them, so you'll have to look after yourselves."

The small children looked at him with wide eyes, and the older ones nodded.

> "When I leave here, lock the door and don't open it for anyone until I instruct you to."
>
> "Can you save them, sir," asked a small voice from the back of the attic.
>
> "I don't know, son, but I will do my best."
>
> "Justine, I want you to wait at the front door and keep watch, see if anyone else comes. There might be more coaches," Michael instructed.
>
> "I am coming with you," she said.

"No. You have to wait for Burbidge and the police, explain to them the gravity of the situation. They'll trust you, since you are Paul's wife. I need to find young Finlay. I am afraid they have kidnapped him from his bed to attend tonight."

Justine nodded, knowing he was right.

"Be careful! Don't do anything heroic until the police get here."

Her words were lost on him. Michael was not paying attention. He was already halfway down the corridor that led to the cellar.

The stone steps down to the cellar were damp, dark, and cold. It felt medieval and ghostly. The smell of wet earth permeated the area, and he wondered how anyone would want to be down in this rat hole. He set the wick in his lamp low, so that there was just enough light to illuminate the step in front of him. Finally, he reached a small door at the bottom of the stairwell, and there was an interior light shining out from underneath it. *This must be the place.* He could hear laughter and the deep voices of men. Yet, he was confused that could hear no terrified children. There was a simple answer to that—Peter always gagged them so the men could talk.

He heard Hayes voice.

"Here we go then, Bishop Smithers. Perhaps you will open the evening and show the new

gentleman what we do to young men who
disobey us."

He heard them all chuckle.

"Take that gag off his mouth" called Donkin, "We want to listen to him enjoy it."

There was another round of loud laughter and applause.

"What's your name, boy?" asked Smithers.

The child didn't answer, and he heard Sedgefield's voice start to bellow orders.

"Whip him, Peter. Whip him until he speaks."

Michael heard a loud struggling followed by shrill protestations.

"Let me go. Let me go!"

He heard the crack of a whip, and the voice screamed in agony. Peter whipped the boy twice again to secure compliance, grunting with effort each time.

"Finlay! Finlay! Kevin Finlay," screamed the boy.

"It has a tongue," shouted Smithers. "Peter, don't put that whip away yet. I have not finished with this little upstart."

Michael's heart clenched. He felt a terrible sensation in his stomach. He fought off the urge to vomit. Subtly, he tried the door, but it was locked from the inside. The men were so distracted with the spectacle that they didn't realise there was anybody outside.

Fearing that Peter and Hayes would kill Kevin if they got the opportunity, Michael charged back up the steps, feelings of anger and peril overtaking any of pain. Desperate, he needed something to open the door with. He ran into one of the store rooms where the coal was kept and picked up a shovel. He ran back to cellar. By now, Kevin was screaming constantly, yet he heard the onlookers deep, delighted laughter.

Michael wedged the metal spade tip between the door and the doorpost to create a lever. He pushed several times. When it didn't budge, he knew he would've to summon the strength to try harder.

In a bold move, the burly but broken Irish man hurled his entire weight against the spade handle. His ribs felt as if they were breaking all over again. By the third time that he did it, he was out of breath, but he heard the wooden door begin to splinter.

Justine, oblivious to her beloved's heroics in the basement, stood at the door waiting for the Mr Burbidge and the police. She was fretting that they were taking too long. Just before full panic set in, she saw a small band of people come around the corner and enter the street. They were carrying lanterns and wooden sticks, led by Mr Burbidge, with Eliza close on his heels. Six policemen followed with one detective inspector.

"Hurry," cried Justine. "They're in the cellar"

Mr Burbidge took the lead with Justine close on his heels. Now, other staff in the building were beginning to wake up at the sound of footsteps and the voices of the police. Doors opened and inquisitive heads emerged.

The steps to the cellar were narrow, and the detective inspector sent his best two men down first, with Mr Burbidge demanding that he accompany them.

> "These are my pupils. This is my school. I have sworn an oath to look after them, and I will fetch them out of that hell hole."

Still struggling in agony with the makeshift lever, mercifully, Michael felt the door give way. He pushed it open, still holding the shovel in his hand.

At first, he saw four gagged children in the corner being held down by Peter's scuttlers to stop them making a run for it. Then he noticed several adult men in the room in various stages of undress. Hayes was standing pouring drinks, while the others sat in comfortable chairs watching Smithers, now standing naked in the middle of the room. Peter was holding down his prey, poor little Finlay.

Michael took two giant steps toward Peter and swung the shovel. It hit him squarely on the chin. Michael gleefully suspected it was broken. Then he brought the shovel down on Peter's head. The thwack made him tumble to the ground where he lay motionless.

Next, he saw Smithers in his state of undress and mauled knee, and was satisfied that he was not capable of putting up much of a fight.

"Get him out of here," shouted Hayes.

Nobody was listening. The scuttlers were already making their escape, now their knucklehead ringmaster, Peter, was unconscious.

With an instinctive defence move, Michael swung round hit Hayes squarely on the head with the shovel. It was then he remembered his earlier desire to kick the hostel manager in the privates. As always, he wanted to keep to his word. As his foe lay open legged on the floor, Michael got ready to swing in his heavy boot. He was too late. The younger and nimbler Kevin Finlay had already pipped him to the post and swooped in to deliver the eyewatering blow.

All about was chaos. It was with considerable relief, Michael saw two uniformed officers coming into the room, led by Burbidge. The policemen had their truncheons out in defence, not knowing the threats they might have to confront—very little it seemed. Donkin, Sedgefield, and Smithers were all cowards, reaching for their clothes to cover their modesty and putting up no resistance whatsoever.

Michael went towards the bound and gagged boys, all terrified and hysterical. He fought to release them and once free, they crowded around him, holding on to him for all they were worth.

"Come lads. It's all over. Things are going to change. I promise. You'll never live through this again."

Michael patted Kevin Finlay on the back.

"Well, done, Kevin. You were very brave. And well done you for finishing off Hayes. I have wanted to kick him in the privates for a long time."

"Really, Sir?" said the little face looking up at him.

Michael winked at the lad and ruffled his hair.

"Really."

The pair of policemen lead Donkin and Sedgefield, two of the most prominent men in the country up the damp steps and into the courtyard, clamping on the handcuffs as they walked.

The last person to emerge from the cellar was Bishop Paul Smithers. As he arose from the darkness, he looked around to see who was watching him. There was only Justine standing at the top of the steps, filled with bitterness and shame. She was disgusted to have his name and disgusted to be associated with him.

Paul looked up at her from the black pit. Whatever sanity he'd left escaped him.

"I should've killed you when I first had the chance," he rasped.

He lurched toward Justine, caught her around the waist and held onto her as tightly as he could. She screamed in terror, knowing what he was capable of.

"Let her go," shouted Michael in agony as he struggled towards the corridor. "Let her go."

He tried to rush to help, but it was pointless. He was far too far away to stop Smithers positioning himself at the top of the stairs, still clamped to Justine despite her putting up another brave struggle. Her husband's knee might have been weak, but his arms were like a vice.

"I will not let her go. She's my wife. For better or worse, till death do us part. You can have her when she is dead," he screeched.

"Let her go, Paul, she has children to take care of, think of them," said Michael, desperately trying to calm the situation."

Paul Smithers put his head back and laughed like a lunatic.

"If you want my wife, come and fetch her."

With that, he used all his might and threw himself back into the dark deep stairwell, pulling Justine into the abyss with him.

"No!" roared Michael, as he heard the blood-curdling thump of their bodies tumbling down the stairs.

In the fall, once again, Paul Smithers had the upper hand, breaking his fall by landing on Justine. Now motionless, he lay on top of her. Michael picked up the evil man and threw him to one side, not caring whether he was dead or alive. He put his ear over Justine's mouth and listened. *Nothing! Not a sound.*

Two more policemen picked up Smithers' naked and limp body and lugged him up to the courtyard on a makeshift stretcher.

Moments later, Michael was convinced he could see that Justine was breathing.

"Justine! Wake up! Wake up!"

"She could not survive a fall like that," muttered Mr Burbidge over Michael's shoulder.

"Well, she'd better survive, because I am not taking her out of this hole in a casket!"

Justine began to groan. He went to take her hand. Her arms flopped arms like a ragdoll. He kissed her face gently like a fairy tale prince hoping to awaken his princess.

"Wake up, Justine. I am not leaving without you. Come my love, we have waited so long to be together. You can't leave me."

His face began to glisten with tears, as he spoke.

"We are going to have a wonderful life, Justine. I am never going to leave you and the girls."

For the first time in years, Michael prayed with great earnest. He praised God when he felt Justine stir in his arms and then begin to mumble.

"Take me home, Michael! I want to go home."

28

THE RESTING PLACE

Justine refused to return to the former family mansion, and Michael didn't want to return to the school. He'd done what was necessary. His job was complete. He'd paid his penance. Michael found a cab for the two of them and made his way to a decent hotel in Manchester, where he reserved two adjoining rooms. From there, he summoned a doctor.

> "Bed rest," ordered the physician. "Thank God she has not broken anything. She seems to be lightly concussed, and has strained ligaments in her neck and back. Other than that, she will recover. Thank God she is alive. It's a miracle."

Now was Michael's opportunity to take care of Justine. For the next few days, they both focused on rest and recuperation. Each night, he bathed her and put her into her warm, clean bed. She was glad to be cocooned in the pretty hotel room, not yet ready to face people.

The scandal attached to the repugnant events at the school had reached far and wide already. The minutia of the events that night was the talk of the town and in the papers, both local and national. Journalists pounded the pavement outside the hotel, desperate to get an interview with the two of them. They were to be disappointed.

"Now, that the ring has been exposed, they'll all beginning to rat on each other, trying to lessen their sentences. The gossiping tongues will have plenty to wag about." said Michael.

"What will happen to them next"

"According to my man in the know, Eddy at the university, they may all hang if proof can be found of their murderous activities. If they're only charged with the kidnapping **and** assault, we are not so sure. It depends on the judge's ruling."

"Is Eddy a professor?"

"No," Michael laughed. "He shelves the returned books at the law library. But he does know his stuff."

"Have you heard from Nel and Father McDermott?"

"Yes, Mrs Bunting refuses to let Nel leave the rectory. She has accepted him as a son, and wants to look after him," Michael laughed. "He doesn't use bad language anymore."

Justine smirked, then her smile faded.

"They murdered little Jono," said Justine fiercely, "Can't we use that against them? They must have all been in on it? Poor mite."

"I am sure they'll try and pin that on Peter. He was their hired henchman. They'll stick together and stitch him up. He will likely hang for that."

"Did the police find the body?"

"Yes, between Edwards and Edwards as you said. It was a very shallow grave. It didn't take much digging to find him. The coroner says the size of the skeleton matched Jono's description and age when he disappeared, so I heard. With a few more tests, I'm sure they'll identify him"

Justine nodded.

"They would never have found him if you had not overheard that awful conversation."

"Michael, we can't leave Jono to be buried at The Flags. That was not where he was destined to be."

"What do you mean?"

"They stole his life, Michael. He wasn't created to be shoved into a shallow mass grave. Let's bring Jono to Liverpool where he can be close to Nel."

"Do you think that will help the lad or set him back? He seems to be settling in nicely. This might upset the applecart" asked Michael.

"More than staring out towards the horizon, his heart aching, wondering where he is?"

He smiled at her. Despite all her many hardships, she was still as compassionate as ever.

"Can I take off your clothes? I need to look over your injuries thoroughly. Doctor's orders," Michael teased gently.

"Of course."

"Can I stay with you for the night?"

"No. You're only next door. People will be talking about us enough already without pouring fuel on the fire—and the management will throw us out!" she exclaimed.

"That's if they catch me," he added with his characteristic cheeky Irish smile.

The next day, Michael received a telegram to say that Shilling Hudson was waiting for him in the lounge.

He quickly brushed his hair, buttoned his shirt, and polished his shoes. He still looked rough around the edges, but it was the best he could manage at short notice.

Justine decided to brave reading the newspaper and was delighted to read her husband's life was hanging in the balance, having never regaining consciousness after the fall.

In the plush reception. Shilling greeted Michael O'Neil with a warm smile.

"Miss Hudson. This is a nice surprise. You might have read I have had a few unpleasant ones of late," he joked, hoping to diffuse any concerns about his morals or lifestyle.

"It's Shilling, remember," she corrected before teasing him a little more. "You look more relaxed than I was expecting considering the number of blows you've had to the head since I last saw you. Perhaps that's why you forgot how I like to be addressed?"

Michael smiled, delighted at her ability to put people at ease, no matter what area of polite society their behaviour had fallen short in. Many people said it was a trait she got from her father.

"I see the story of the school has been emblazoned in the press for days."

"Yes, it's up to the courts now."

"Let me be direct, if I may. I want to take over that Corning Street school, Michael. I want to give those boys a real life."

"They can be a handful," he warned. "It'll never be the Eton for engineers."

"Yes, I do know. We'd many challenges in Birmingham—we still do."

"Well, then I cannot offer you any advice about running an educational facility. I am just a lowly teacher."

She gave him an encouraging smile.

"I wanted to take over the school to nurture the children," shilling revealed, "but now my motive has changed a little."

"How so?" asked Michael.

"I want those boys to know that not all rich people are evil, that becoming rich is not evil, and that they too can be great men, good men—industrial pioneers."

"What do you need from me?"

"Michael, I need a good manager, and I am prepared to pay you an excellent salary."

"Mr Burbidge is an experienced headmaster."

"I disagree. Mr Burbidge did not know what was happening under his very roof. He is not good enough for me. Those children are from the streets, and I can guarantee that they have no faith in Mr Burbidge, even with the legal system taking on their abusers."

"Shilling, I can understand your conviction in the place, but I am not the man to help you. I have other challenges to face."

"They must be very important if you choose to turn down an offer like this one."

"Yes, I am becoming a father."

"How lovely. When is the baby due? And the wedding date?"

"No, you don't understand. I am marrying their mother. Rosie and Hope are already here."

Shilling put her head back and gave a loud sincere laugh.

"Oh Michael, how wonderful. That is far more appealing than living in Angel Meadow, I'm sure."

Shilling stood up, and they shook hands.

"You can write to me for advice."

"Thank you, Michael. I will do that."

Michael watched Shilling Hudson walk away. He could only admire her. She had a presence that no one could ignore. He would never forget the bold green eyes and that scar on her face—earned when she too threw herself in harm's way to protect a defenceless little urchin boy.

*

A respectful group stood under a large tree in the convent garden. It was a peaceful place filled with birds and small animals, giving it a life of its own.

Father McDermott led the service. The onlookers watched the coffin being lowered into the earth. Nel was bitterly sad, and tears ran down his little face. His little heart broke at the knowledge that he would never see his brother again. Justine explained to him that he would be always close to Jono and could speak to him whenever he wished. She reassured him although he might be gone in body, he wouldn't be gone in mind.

Mrs Bunting put her arms around the boy and held him close. She wiped the tears off his face. Michael had ordered a small headstone made which they put next to the grave. The young lad patted the smooth black marble with heart wrenching pride.

Michael kneeled in front of him.

> "Do you see that headstone Nel? You might have lost Jono once, but you will always find that headstone here, and so you'll never lose him again."

Nel nodded, and smiled at Michael for his kind gesture, but his tear-stained face was still pale and sad. Michael hugged him. He whispered some private words of comfort.

> "I think you have a good mother in Mrs Bunting. She'll fight in your corner when you need it."

"Aye," said Nel.

Michael stood up and gave the lad a smile.

"You know where to send your letters to me, don't you?"

"Yes," answered Nel.

"If you ever need me, you can contact me, and I will always come and help you."

"Even if you are far away?" asked Nel.

"Yes, even if I am very far away."

The colour started to return to Nel's cheeks a little, and the faintest hint of a smile.

29

TOMORROW AS GOOD AS TODAY

The sun was setting over a field of purple lavender. The last light of the day was high lighting golden fields of barley and a vineyard with the fattest purple grapes. In the distance was a large faded Tuscan villa built from local sandstone.

Next to the villa was a barn. It was filled with paraphernalia that only Justine could identify. She'd settled quickly in her world of artists and music. Her soul was at peace. Once again, none of her clothes matched and everything she wore was an uncoordinated and colourful mess. Her dark hair was tied back in a clip and hung down her back in wild curls. Her black eyes sparkled.

It was a warm evening. Rosie and Hope were in the pond standing under the fountain. The water was crystal clear, and they squealed with delight as they splashed in the late sunshine. Two dogs were barking, eager to participate in the fun.

A tall, dark man sat the veranda and looked out on his farm. They'd worked hard. The cellars were teeming of casks of the most sought-after wine in the world, with this year's bumper harvest soon to double that amount.

He watched Justine close her studio door, her dark hair aglow in the setting sun. The two children climbed out of the fountain and ran toward their mother.

They all looked toward the house and waved at Michael relaxing in his favourite bench on the veranda. His heart soared. Of all the beauty of his surroundings, these three women were the glittering jewels in the scenery—and his life. He adored them.

Rosie and Hope O'Neil clambered into his lap.

"Will you read us a story, Papa?"

"Yes, I always do."

"Now!" they begged, dragging him inside, taking one arm each.

More than an hour later, Justine went into the children's bedroom. Michael was sitting on the rocking chair reading merrily, as the girls were lying in their beds listening intently.

She bent over and gave him a lingering kiss on the soft skin by his ear.

"I am waiting for you," she whispered.

Michael speeded up his pace and quickly finished the chapter, without the girls noticing.

Justine lay in Michael's arms, and her one hand was caressing his broad chest. He looked down at her and smiled.

"If you had your life over, is there anything that you would change?" whispered Justine.

"No," replied Michael.

"What if we met earlier and never had any troubles?"

"Well, then I wouldn't have Rosie and Hope, would I?"

Justine smiled.

"Do you think that every day is going to be as good as today?"

"You have been asking me that question for five years, and what do I always say to you."

"I can't remember," Justine quipped playfully.

"Yes, Justine, tomorrow is going to be as good as today."

.